THE WAY THE RHUBARB CRUMBLES

John Bayer

Melicrate Press

Dedication

Although the characters in this book are not based on specific people, the fictional town of Kirby, North Dakota would not exist without the inspiration of the wonderful folks of Divide County and the town of Crosby.

This book is dedicated to them, and specifically to the late John Fosland who I miss greatly.

There are no secrets in a small town.

There are known facts, and there are the facts that haven't come out just yet.

That is all.

1

"Someone ought to murder Calvin Lystad, then" a voice declared, as Jim Rosdahl entered the post office. Jim wore his light fall jacket, the one he wore on days when the temperature in Kirby, North Dakota fluctuates anywhere between 25 and 50 degrees Fahrenheit. The current temperature this September morning was 45 degrees – about 25 degrees below average for this time of year.

The youthful 52-year-old entered the Kirby post office with a large manila envelope in his hand and an entire universe of thoughts in his head.

The voice in question belonged to Ardis Knutson. She was speaking for the benefit of her best friend, Ardis Knudsvig – commonly referred to around town as "the other Ardis" – and for the postmaster, Candy Gillund.

"Uff da, Ardis," the other Ardis said, "be careful what you say and where you say it. Jim might not know you're joking."

Knutson (said with a hard K, "Keh-noot-son) had been looking at Candy while she spoke and had not noticed Jim come in. Ardis Knutson was older than dirt and her peripheral vision had departed sometime around the Lincoln Administration. Ardis Knutson slowly rotated her body toward the door – her ability to move her neck having also abandoned her some time back. She gave Jim a slight smile before returning to her usual scowl.

"Ya, who says I'm joking?" she said in an accent that was one part Norwegian, two parts Canadian (minus the "eh") and three parts "then," "now" and "ya." The standard accent in this region.

"She was joking," the other (and younger) Ardis assured Jim as she smiled and shook her head. Ardis Knudsvig (another hard K) was born a few years after dirt and still possessed some neck mobility.

"Good morning," Jim said. "I'm sure she was." Jim gave them a reassuring smile that said, *I know how Ardis can get. I don't hold anything she says against her. I understand.*

In truth, Jim had no idea what Ardis had said. He had other thoughts to contend with. When you own the local newspaper, people assume that you're always on high alert, looking for stories, quotes, evidence. But really, sometimes you're replaying last night's game in your head and convincing yourself that the Vikings still could have pulled it out if they hadn't wasted all their timeouts.

"Morning. I mean it," Ardis Knutson said. "This town would be better off without Calvin Lystad. Someone ought to just finish him off, then."

"What has our illustrious mayor done now?" Jim asked.

"You're the newspaper man. You tell us." Candy said. The stocky, 40-something postmaster always had a smile in her voice, though no one had ever seen one on her lips. She placed a postal sticker onto a small package before her. "That's $11.40, Ardis."

"Everyone knows, if you want the news you read the paper. If you want to know what's really going on, you go to the post office." Jim said.

Jim was a charmer. Candy's eyes smiled, while her mouth held onto its trademark scowl. Ardis Knudsvig let out a small, almost girlish giggle. Ardis, who had never married, had always had a small crush on Jim's father, Marlin Rosdahl, and some residue of it transferred to Jim after Marlin's death.

Ardis Knutson had finally spun her way back to facing the counter. "Eleven dollars! Uff da! Are you delivering my package in a gold-plated truck?"

"Same old story," Candy said, answering Jim's question and ignoring Ardis's. "Calvin Lystad continues his campaign to become supreme dictator of Kirby. The fight over the hospital tax. Trying to steal Bud Legaard's land. And the stuff with the daycare."

"I suppose these things will work themselves out eventually." Jim was ever the diplomat.

"Ya, it'll work out when he's dead," Ardis Knutson having forked over her $11.40 was feeling even more foul-tempered than before.

"I'm sure there are less violent way to resolve all of these issues," Jim said.

Ardis Knudsvig nodded. "I agree. Too early in the day for talk of blood and guts."

"Murder doesn't have to be bloody," the senior Ardis assured the group. "If you poison Calvin, there's no blood. And the bonus is you don't have to be there when he dies."

"Run Calvin over with your car," Candy offered as a sort of rebuttal. "Don't you want to see the terror on his face?"

"Oh dear," was all the other Ardis could offer.

Jim spoke up. "But is a car tactile enough?" he said with a roguish smile. Jim enjoyed playing the instigator from time to time.

"What do you mean?" Candy asked.

Ardis Knutson answered for Jim, "If you're going to go that route, you want to have the full experience. Stab Calvin, and then you feel like it was actually you killing him and not some machine."

Candy defended her preferred method of murder. "I think when the car goes over Calvin like a human speed bump, you'd get whatever satisfaction you needed, sure."

"Gun," Ardis Knudsvig, who had moved off to the side a bit, spoke up.

Jim and Candy turned to her. In time, Ardis Knutson rotated to look at her friend as well.

"Poisoning is too unpredictable. You wouldn't know until too late if you'd been successful. A car accident is too public. You don't want the risk of being seen. Unless you know what you're doing, stabbing might take quite a few attempts. And you have to be able to overpower the other person. A gun is the way to go." The other Ardis, it seemed, had overcome her squeamishness.

"Just so you know, ladies" Jim said, "I charge $500 for alibis. Also, I need advance warning."

Ardis Knudsvig gave her girlish giggle.

Ardis Knutson shook her head as much as was possible for her. "Uff da. I'm too old to go around killing people. Murder is a young man's game."

"Ya, no. I don't know," Jim said as he looked out the window. "Here comes Hazel. Let's ask her."

Hazel Lystad was Calvin Lystad's ample wife. The eyes of the two Ardises grew wide.

"Uff da! We should go," said the younger Ardis as she gently strong-armed her best friend toward the door. "I need to get some things at the Yarn Barn. Have a good day."

Jim handed Candy the manila envelope that he had been holding.

"I don't see Hazel Lystad outside."

"My mistake," Jim said with a smirk. "Another stack of mail for Claudette."

Candy looked at the address on the envelope. "That wife of yours has been in Bismarck some time now. Has that grandbaby arrived yet?"

"Not yet. Right now Claudette's helping Ashley get everything in the house ready. Nesting I think they call it."

"When's she coming back?" Candy asked. Like all good reporters, Candy Gillund was continually looking for the truth beneath the story. Even if there wasn't one. She looked at her monitor, then said, "$4.75."

"She'll stay for a bit to help the kids out with the new baby. After that."

"No problems with the baby, I hope."

"Claudette's just overly anxious. First time grandparents,

you know."

"Steve and Ashley aren't having troubles? Sometimes the pressure of a new baby gets to couples."

Jim shook his head.

"Will she be back in time for the lutefisk supper, then?" Each year in late fall and early winter, communities throughout North Dakota hold celebratory dinners dedicated to a mushy, lye-soaked, cod delicacy called lutefisk.

"That's nearly two months away," Jim said, handing Candy exact change.

"I need to know if I'm losing my assistant chairwoman. It takes time to find replacements. People don't help out with things the way they used to."

"I'll have Claudette call you. I'd better get going; I'm late for the morning meeting."

Candy looked at the wall clock. 10:09. "You still have five minutes." Newspapers have to work closely with the post office, so Candy knew the work schedule at *The Kirby Crier* pretty well.

"Oh good. I'll be on time for once," Jim said with a smile. He offered his good-bye and walked out the door.

Candy went to her desk in the back, disappointed. Sometimes the fisherman makes his catch. Sometimes he gets one on the line, but the fish manages to get free before it can be reeled in. Other times, the fisherman senses that the fish are there, even if they never bite. Candy Gillund felt there was a big catch nearby; she had simply used the wrong bait.

Aside

Welcome to Clark County located in the northwest corner of North Dakota. A county so small if you blink, you'll miss it. A place so small you might not be able to find it on a map. So small, it's almost as if it doesn't exist, as if some guy had just made the whole place up.

The seat and largest city in Clark County, with a population of a whopping 1,042 people, is the bustling metropolis of Kirby. Kirby has it all: a grocery store, a drug store, a single screen movie theater, two bars, five places to eat, a gym, and seven insurance agencies. If you have a fast food hankering, you'll need to drive one hour south to Williston, ND to get to a McDonald's; unless you have your passport, then it's only thirty-five minutes north to the one in Estevan, Saskatchewan.

Main Street looks like something built on a Hollywood studio backlot used for any script that calls for "Small Town, U.S.A." Kirby is largely made up of people of Norwegian descent, with Belgians coming in a distant second. Germans take the bronze. The people in Kirby are very friendly, as long as you're asking about the weather and not about them. If you're asking for the dirt on other people though, they get even friendlier.

Farming is the lifeblood of Kirby, of Clark County, of North Dakota. The majority of the nation's wheat and canola come from North Dakota. The Kirby Co-op Grain Elevator is located at the intersection of Main Street and the train tracks at the center of town. Agriculture – both metaphorically and literally – is the center of it all in Kirby.

Kirby is on the northern edge of the Bakken Formation; that's where they found all that fracking oil. Starting around 2010, the cities and towns in the Bakken Formation were transformed as oil workers began flooding into an area without the roads, housing, restaurants, and all around infrastructure to handle them. The oil boom brought lots of money flooding into the state, which is good because it cost a lot of money to get the state to a place where it could accommodate the growth.

By 2014, the boom was ending. The price of oil dropped to a point where it wasn't worth the investment to keep building and operating all those drills in North Dakota. Cities in the heart of the boom, like Williston, Watford City, and Tioga felt the greatest impact from the slowdown. Being on the outskirts, Kirby was affected both by the boom and the bust but was not completely transformed by either.

But this is a story of another kind...

2

The Kirby Crier newspaper has been serving the healthy and hearty people of Kirby, North Dakota since 1918. Knute Rosdahl and Ernest Vigness began putting out *The Clark County Tribune* in 1915; but Knute and Ernest had some sort of falling out, so three years later, Knute Rosdahl started *The Crier*. Competition – or perhaps the loss of Knute – proved fatal for the *Tribune*, and it closed its doors two years later. *The Kirby Crier* enjoyed great success. In 1963, Knute sold the newspaper to his middle son, Marlin Rosdahl. In 1993, on the eve of celebrating 30 years of ownership, Marlin suffered a brain aneurysm and died. His son Jim – who with his wife Claudette and their two sons were in town for a visit and to celebrate Marlin's milestone – became the *de facto* owner and lead reporter of *The Kirby Crier*. Jim and Claudette enrolled the boys in Clark County Elementary School. Claudette drove the nine and a half hours back to The Cities (Minneapolis/St. Paul), sold the house and said goodbye to all of their friends, while Jim relearned all of the lessons of the newspaper game that his father had labored to teach him so many years before.

The Crier is a weekly newspaper written and laid out each Tuesday in Kirby and then sent electronically to the printing plant in the big city of Minot (population around 45,000). And every Tuesday evening, Allan Borreson (occasional photographer for the Crier) makes the two-hour drive to Minot – come rain or snow or more snow – picks up the newspapers, then makes the two-hour drive back to Kirby. By Wednesday morning, the paper is neatly tucked into each subscriber's box (Kirby does not have mail delivery; every resident has a box down at the post office).

Jim had owned the paper for over twenty years now. In that

time, he had been on time for the Wednesday morning meeting perhaps a half-dozen times. Counting today.

That staff of *The Crier* consisted of Brian Jacobson, reporter; Layla Hedahl who designed the ads and laid out the paper, and Toni Fagerbakke, a jack of all trades. Toni's job title was News Associate, or something equally innocuous-sounding; her actual job was taking care of all the things that needed to be taken care of that weren't being taken care of by someone else.

Although Jim was on time for once, when he arrived his staff had already gathered around the small table in the back which served as both the conference table and the break room table. Toni was in the midst of recounting the funeral for Miriam Larson that she had attended over the weekend.

"My sister and I served as pall bearers, along with Andrea Dhuyvetter and Miriam's nieces from Bowbells," Toni informed them.

"There were no male pall bearers?" Brian asked.

"Nope. Miriam gave very specific instructions." Toni leaned forward, as if conveying government secrets. "She said, 'Men wouldn't take me out when I was alive-'"

"I won't let them take me out when I'm dead." Jim completed the thought. It was an old joke, but it still got a laugh out of Layla. Toni sat back with a smile of satisfaction. Brian seemed confused by the whole thing.

"So what have we got, then?" Jim asked as he sat down. Having put one issue to bed the day before, the Wednesday morning meeting served as the launching off point for the next week's newspaper.

Brian consulted his notepad. "They're doing that 'don't text and drive' program at the high school tomorrow. Thought I'd go down and take some pictures. Thought I might also talk to students about this closed campus proposal floating around."

"It would be good to also get Dr. Davis's perspective on that." Jim said.

"Okay." Brian let out a subtle sigh. Brian enjoyed interviewing students — he found them easy to talk to and they would pretty much agree to say anything he needed them to say to fit into the story that he had already decided to tell. Adults intimidated Brian. He went into every interview feeling as if he were about to climb a steep hill wearing sandals. Dr. Victor Davis, the school superintendent, was Mount Kilimanjaro.

"How's the story on the swimming pool renovation going?" Jim asked.

"It's coming." Brian answered. "Spoke to Mickey Kilroy last night." Mickey Kilroy, the owner of the Burger Shack, served on the park board overseeing the renovation of the community swimming pool. "I'll be able to get about 12 inches out of it."

Jim had hoped the story would fill up more space in the paper than that, but he would take what he could get from Brian. "Sounds good," Jim lied.

"Mickey wants to read the story before we print it," Brian said.

"He always does," Jim said. "Kindly inform him once again that *The Crier* has never and will never abdicate editorial control to the subject of our reporting."

"That's too many big words for Mickey to understand," Toni offered.

Jim continued to address Brian, "A firm 'no' will suffice."

Just then Toni caught sight through the back window of Eugenia Ingqvist shuffling towards her car. "Shut up, everyone. Show's starting."

Eugenia lived in a small house across the alley from *The Crier*. The meeting stopped while the staff watched Eugenia get into the ocean liner she called her car and attempt to back it out into the alley. Eugenia was old — she had once babysat for Moses — and by all accounts a menace behind the wheel. Although the house had an attached garage, Eugenia never parked her car there except in winter. The garage door was bent across several of its slats, where two months prior, Eugenia had mistakenly placed her car into drive instead of park, and succeeded in colliding at 18 MPH into her closed garage door. The staff had, unfortunately, missed out on that spectacle. Since then, the staff was on high alert, hoping to catch the next show. In the span of four minutes and 37 seconds, Eugenia managed the Herculean task of pulling her car out of the driveway and heading down the alley out of view. She destroyed one of her neighbor's – Gladys Rosdahl – chokecherry bushes in the process. "Mom never liked that bush anyway," Jim assured the others.

The meeting resumed. "City council this week." Jim read off his own notepad.

"That's tonight?" Brian asked. Brian had been the reporter for *The Crier* for nine years. In those nine years, the city council meeting had always been on the second Wednesday of the month. "Judith and I were planning to have dinner in Estevan tonight."

A request hovered in the air. During Brian's first days on staff, Jim would pluck the request out of the air. But that had ended pretty quickly. It was Jim's paper, so he would do whatever work needed to get done; but he would at least make Brian sweat it out a little.

"Can you cover the meeting?" Brian asked, after Jim did not fill in the blank himself. "Or I can just get notes from Lois tomorrow morning."

"There's a lot on the agenda. We shouldn't rely on the city clerk's notes. They're going to discuss the new daycare."

"Why is the council still dragging their feet on that?" Layla asked. "Shooting ourselves in the foot."

"Everyone knows we need one; but some people don't think the city should have to pay for it," Jim said in his nonpartisan way.

"Yip. Well, some people are stupid. If I didn't have mom to look after Mason during the day, I wouldn't be able to work."

"You should come to the meeting and express your opinion," Jim said.

"Oh, I don't care what they do." Layla said. Layla's last name was Hedahl, a good Norwegian name. Like the majority of Kirby residents, she was herself a good Norwegian, from a long line of good Norwegians. When a good Norwegian says, "I don't care what they do" what she means is "I don't care to make a spectacle of myself."

"Dennis Anderson will be at the meeting," Toni informed the group. Dennis Anderson was the director of Kirby's hospital, St. Eustace; and not a fan of Kirby's mayor. "Calvin Lystad won't put the hospital tax initiative on the November ballot." Toni was telling the group what they already knew.

"I don't think he can do that," Layla said, "legally."

"Well, he seems to be doing it," returned Jim.

Layla took a sip of coffee before replying. "Sometimes I just want to shake Calvin and say 'what are you thinking'?"

"Maybe you should ask Hazel," Jim suggested. Hazel Lystad and Layla's mother were cousins.

"Maybe you should ask Abby, now," Toni suggested. Conjecture around town was that Calvin Lystad and Abby Quicke were having an affair.

Jim smiled and took a sip of his coffee.

"Judith and I are going up to Canada tonight," Brian reminded the group.

"I'll cover the meeting," Jim assured him.

The conversation detoured from there. Several minutes were occupied with speculation about the nature of Dennis Anderson's hair. Brian and Layla were firmly on the side that Dennis wore a toupee. Jim and Toni believed it was just so terribly styled that it gave off that impression. Layla ventured a guess that the conversation at the city council meeting would get so heated, that Dennis's toupee would fly off in the middle of a tirade. Brian bet her five dollars – two to one odds – that it would not occur. Jim would go to the meeting and report back.

There was a sound at the other end of the building; the sound of the front door opening and closing. There being no clear line of sight from the back, Toni left the table to see if a customer might have come in.

"What else have we got?" Jim asked.

"I saw a V of geese yesterday," Layla offered.

"Uff da! Already?" Jim said.

Brian looked puzzled. "What?"

"It'll be an early winter," Layla said.

"It will?" Brian asked.

"Geese don't lie."

Jim addressed Brian "We could do something on how that might affect crops. Why don't you talk to Abel Bunsen and see what he thinks."

"Abel Bunsen hates talking to me," Brian said, in that way a four year old says he doesn't want to eat his broccoli.

"But at least he *will* talk to you," Jim countered. As a rule, farmers are not interested in granting interviews. Norwegian farmers would rather have elective surgery than go on the record. The only larger "get" for a newspaper reporter would be a sit down interview with Sasquatch.

With the meeting concluded, Jim, Layla, and Brian walked back to the front of the building. Jim went into his tiny office, while Brian and Layla returned to their desks in the common area.

Toni was behind the counter. On the other end was a shriveled up old man named Bud Legaard. Bud looked angry, but to be fair he always looked angry. Bud looked angry even when he was smiling. He looked angry even when he was asleep, a fact to which anyone who attended St. Mary Catholic Church with him could attest.

"I've been a subscriber for sixty years, sure enough. You shouldn't be able to just cancel my paper, you know."

"I'm trying to explain," Toni tried to explain, "your subscription ran out, but we can renew it today. Do you have

$41?"

"I haven't received the paper for two weeks. Just canceled. No notice. No how do you do." Bud cried out with all his might, in case the people next door at the dentist's office might be interested in what he had to say.

"I did mail out a renewal card last month." Toni said, the tone and volume of her voice nearly matching Bud's. "But like I said, it's no problem renewing you today."

Bud grumbled something to himself, reached into his pocket, and pulled out a wad of cash. He found two $20 bills and threw them on the counter. Toni took the money.

"Do you have another dollar?" she asked.

"What for?"

"The newspaper is $41 a year."

"It's 40," Bud assured her.

"The subscription rate went up by one dollar this year."

Bud put the wad of cash back into his pocket. "Ya, I've been a subscriber to this paper for sixty years. I advertise my yard sales in this paper. I -"

Jim joined Toni behind the counter. As much as he got a kick out of Bud Legaard's curmudgeon act, he could tell his news associate was on the verge of losing it. "Forty dollars is fine, Bud. We'll get you all squared away, now. Here's this week's paper if you need."

Jim grabbed a paper from the stack on the counter and handed it to Bud. Bud placed the paper under his arm, turned around and walked out the door, grumbling to himself the entire way. Jim thought he could make out the words "unprofessional," "circus," and "sixty years."

Toni turned to her boss. "Thank you. Another minute of that, and you'd been calling the sheriff to break up a fight between an old man and a beautiful young woman."

"You're welcome," Jim said with a smile. "Of course, I'll have to take that dollar out of your next paycheck."

Brian cleared his throat to get Jim's attention. "Speaking

of the sheriff. I forgot in our meeting: the new deputy started this week. Aidan Black. He's coming in at 2:00 today for an interview."

"You'll be here?" Jim asked.

Brian was offended. "Of course, I'll be here."

3

Brian was nowhere to be found that afternoon when the new sheriff's deputy arrived at *The Crier*.

"I'm here for an interview, I guess." He addressed Toni whose desk was nearest the customer counter. The deputy removed his heavy coat; he looked young and athletic in his uniform – a sharp contrast to the other four members of the Clark County Sheriff's Office.

"Oh, hello," Toni said with a smile as she turned her head slightly to the right, to highlight her left side (her best side) to its fullest. "Can I take your coat?" This offer far exceeded the usual level of customer service that Toni provided.

"Thanks, I'll just hold onto it."

Jim came out of his tiny office – when you're the big boss, you get 3' x 6' room with a pocket door that doesn't work – and walked to the front to meet the new deputy. Jim made a mental note to have a talk with Brian Jacobson.

Jim extended his hand. "You must be Aidan Black. Jim Rosdahl."

Aidan took his hand. "Aidan Gray, actually."

"Well, I knew it was a color." Jim amended his mental note to "fire Brian Jacobson." Jim had used up quite a stack of mental sticky notes over the last four years regarding the fate of Mr. Jacobson.

Jim led Aidan to the conference table at the back of the building. Toni watched them leave for the back. . . well, she watched *one* of them.

The *Crier* building was basically one big, narrow room, save for Jim's office, the bathroom and a storage closet. By virtue of being furthest away from the front desk, the conference table was what passes for private in a small town.

"When did you get in?"

"Tuesday."

Jim offered Aidan a seat, then sat on the opposite end of the table.

"Yesterday or a week ago Tuesday?"

"I guess it was just yesterday." Jim could almost see Aidan's head swimming. "Moving," was all Aidan offered as an explanation.

"A bit overdressed for the occasion, aren't you?"

"Oh, the uniform? I just got off my shift."

Jim shifted his eyes to the chair where Aidan had laid his coat. "I was referring to the winter parka."

"In case you hadn't noticed," Aidan said, "It's cold outside."

Jim laughed at this. "It's only September."

"I can't feel my toes." Aidan joked, but didn't joke.

Jim laughed again. "You might want to get a second parka to put over that one come January."

With the obligatory weather conversation out the way, the two men got down to the interview. Jim asked the standard questions: *How long have you been in law enforcement? Where are you from? What do you think of our little burg?* Aidan gave the standard answers: *Almost five years, Tucson, Kirby is beautiful and the people are friendly. And it's cold.*

The two men got on from the start. The friendly interview morphed into more personal conversation. But still friendly.

"Thirty-one is pretty young to be divorced, isn't it?" Jim asked.

"Not really," Aidan assured him, "But thirty-one is pretty young to be divorced twice."

Jim raised an eyebrow. A curious, rather than judgmental eyebrow.

"I'm an overachiever." Aidan stated simply. "What, you don't have divorce here?"

"Of course we do." Jim said.

But not a lot. People tend to stay together in rural North Dakota. It's nice to have someone beside you through the long, harsh winter; if not for love, at least for the extra body heat.

"They didn't warn me how probing this interview was going to get."

"Sorry, I'll switch gears," Jim said. "Tell me this, how old were you when you finally stopped wetting the bed."

Aidan laughed, a good hearty laugh. "Let's keep some mystery between us, Jim. I'll hold one or two things secret."

Jim shook his head. "You're in a small town now, officer. There's no such thing as secrets."

"Fine. I stopped wetting the bed at 23."

"That's kind of late."

"Reason my first marriage ended."

Jim laughed, a more conservative, self-conscious (North Dakota) laugh.

The back door opened and Gladys Rosdahl entered carrying two pies tins. "How's it looking out there?" Jim asked.

"No wind today," Gladys replied. "That's good."

"This is the new deputy, Aidan Gray. This is my mother, Gladys."

"Hello." said Aidan, "Nice to meet you."

"Uff da! Is that your coat?" Gladys offered as a greeting. She turned to her son, "I thought you were coming over for dinner. I made a crumble." Gladys set one of the pie tins on the counter.

"Did I say I was coming over for lunch?"

For Gladys Bakke Rosdahl, lunch was dinner and dinner was supper. Gladys Bakke Rosdahl was what the kids call "old school."

"You didn't say you weren't."

"Can't argue with that logic. Rhubarb?"

"Of course." Gladys turned to Aidan to inform him, "I grow it myself."

"Who's the other one for?" Jim asked.

"This one's a pie. For Abby. She likes my rhubarb."

Abby Quicke, 58, was boisterous and demonstrative and open. And nearly everyone in town believed that she was carrying on with the mayor. People kept their distance. Gladys wasn't exactly friends with Abby, but she considered the rumor utter foolishness. She would have no part in the besmirching of Abby Quicke's name. In response, Gladys Rosdahl made pie. Baking as an act of rebellion.

Jim called out to the front of the building. "Hey guys, there's rhubarb crumble back here if anyone wants some."

Toni was half way to the table before Jim had finished his sentence. Layla came soon afterward, with Brian close behind. *He's always here when there's food*, Jim thought, *I've really got to fire that guy.*

Aidan rose from the table and grabbed his inappropriate coat.

"Stay for some," Jim said to Aidan.

"Yes, please do," Toni agreed a little too eagerly.

"I'd better not," he said, patting his nonexistent gut.

Aidan made his goodbyes and left out the front. Toni watched him leave.

Gladys served up a helping to Layla with a sour expression on her face. "Who doesn't stay for rhubarb? Uff da!"

Aside

Uff da is a Norwegian-American term that means, well, "uff da." It's hard to explain exactly what it means. If it's winter and you slip on the ice but somehow manage not to fall, you would say "UFF DA," meaning "that was a close one." If you slip on the ice and still fall on your butt, you would say a more subdued "uff da" to mean "well, I went and done it now." If the zombie apocalypse came and you were surrounded on all sides by the living dead who only want to eat your brains and you have absolutely no means of escape, you would say "UFF da" which is loosely translated into "we've really stepped into some horse-shucks here."

Uff da is the word that you say when you just can't say anything else. It's the Scandinavian equivalent to the Yiddish phrase "Oy vey."

Uff da is never a celebratory exclamation. The closest it comes to that is when you are extremely overweight and you say "uff da" after you've managed to successfully lift yourself out of your chair. That's it. Norwegians are not by nature a celebratory people. Celebration draws too much attention. Norwegians like to remain unseen, hidden, and stealthy. That's why so many famous ninjas have been Norwegian.

4

Small town city council meetings are, generally speaking, a great place for an insomniac to find some relief. Occasionally, the council's action on some issue will stir up the ire of a particular person or group; but those confrontations were still nothing you couldn't sleep through if you concentrated.

This was not the type of meeting awaiting those who attended the Kirby City Council meeting in September. For about a year, The Kirby City Council – led by the indomitable (and insufferable) Mayor Calvin Lystad – had made one ire-stirring decision after another. All of these issues were coming to a head at this meeting.

When Jim entered the Kathleen Rosdahl Room at Clark County Elementary School, he was five minutes late, his usual MO. Calvin Lystad was just calling the meeting to order. Jim looked around for an empty seat, but all twenty chairs that had been set out were occupied. The chair closest to the window – and farthest from Jim – was occupied by Gladys Rosdahl. Jim gave a quick wave to his mother. Being a demonstrative Norwegian, Gladys nodded her head slightly in reply.

Jim, along with about a dozen other folks, had to stand during the meeting. He was forced to stand in the doorway, therefore being doubly inconvenienced.

Chairs could have been grabbed from another classroom, but weren't. At some point, time immemorial, Lois Pedersen had determined that twenty chairs was the correct number to set out for the city council meeting. And nothing – not even the empirical evidence that they needed more chairs – was going to modify that number. Lois Pedersen became city clerk on her 30th birthday – some 31 years and change ago – and in all her time serving as city clerk things worked fine and she had no intention of changing it now, thank you very much. No one bothered to argue with her because, well, she was Lois Pedersen.

The Kathleen Rosdahl Room had been donated to the elementary school – and the community, really – by Jim's father Marlin in the 1980s as a tribute to Marlin's mother, Kathleen. Over the years, the Kathleen Rosdahl Room had become the default meeting space for many of the area's organizations and committees. This included the city council, seeing as the city government building was too small to hold its own meetings.

The room was a decent size, able to fit about 70 or 80 people comfortably. Less, if you insisted on setting up the city council's long table in the middle of the room – as Lois Pedersen always did – cutting off much of the space from spectators. In that case, you could squeeze 30 or 35 people into the room uncomfortably.

"Let's get this thing underway, okay," Calvin Lystad began. The room got quiet quickly, as the audience tried to hear the mayor. Calvin spoke loudly enough, but his words always seemed to hover around his mouth, too tired to travel the distance to the listener's ear; so it often took some effort to make him out.

For this very important meeting, the laid back Calvin Lystad, 67, had dressed in overalls that showcased his stomach to its optimal roundness, and a ball cap that read "Empire Oil." Calvin had been raised on a farm – his older brother Paul still raised winter wheat and canola there – and he retained the look and demeanor of a farmer, though he had been a "city boy" for some time now. He hardly came across as a lightning rod of loathing or vitriol. Historically, very few evil dictators have worn overalls.

"First item is to discuss," Calvin read from the agenda, "the proposed daycare." Calvin's head turned to his left, where council members Andrea Dhuyvetter and Jon Knutson sat. Not seeing who he wanted, he turned to his right to see council member Ryan Peterson and city clerk Lois Pedersen. "I thought we killed this thing already."

"We did turn down their assistance request back in April," Lois confirmed.

"And now they've filed another request," Ryan Peterson said. "We have to at least look at it, Mr. Mayor." At 46, Ryan Peterson was the youngest member of the council. Ryan carried the air of a politician. He always wore a suit to council meetings, he always smiled, and he always spoke diplomatically. Ryan was unlike Calvin in just about every way imaginable, and he disliked Calvin in just about every way imaginable.

"You haven't killed a thing," Val Bakke announced from the audience as she rose from her seat. "The daycare is alive and well. We need to build a new daycare, and we're going to build a new daycare."

"We don't need it, Val."

"We most certainly do."

"Three years ago, I would have agreed with you," Calvin said. "The place was overrun with people from the oilfield. New families with kids. But the oil is gone now, then."

"We need a larger facility, Calvin. We have a waiting list right now with 9 names on it. Locals. Stay-at-home moms who want to get back in the workforce. Single parents. Two income families that have to leave the kids with grandma and grandpa."

"Val, that's what grandparents are for, now."

The blood boiling in Val's veins was transforming the color of her round face from a yellow onion to a beet. "You, sir, are an ass."

"Careful, Mrs. Bakke. Don't make me call the sheriff on you." Calvin said with a smile. Val was married to the Clark County Sheriff, Tor Bakke.

Councilwoman Andrea Dhuyvetter, 49, a short and spunky redhead, spoke up before things could get too out of hand. "Val, how is this request different than the one you made back in April?"

The daycare was seeking less money this time around. Funds were coming in from other places – private donations, grants from the state and charitable funds. The groundbreaking for the new facility could take place as early as the spring, if they could just get that last boost from the city.

Several other members of the community weighed in, all in support of the new facility. Ryan Peterson and Andrea Dhuyvetter were in favor of offering the city's assistance – Andrea because she saw the value that it would have for the community; Ryan because he liked to stand opposite of wherever the overall-clad mayor stood. It was unclear where the other city council member, Jon Knutson, stood on this (or most any other) issue.

Sensing that the tide was against him, Calvin convinced the council to table the issue until next month, so that everyone would have an opportunity to study the request more fully. A month was probably enough time for Calvin to strong arm Andrea Dhuyvetter into changing her mind.

Jim looked at his watch: 7:43. It had taken over a half-hour to discuss one agenda item. And they hadn't even acted on that item! In his heart of hearts, Jim Rosdahl had always believed he would live to be 100 years old. Now, he was starting to suspect that when that day arrived, he would still be in this meeting. Thankfully, the next few items on the agenda were your more standard, snooze-worthy city council meeting fare. They were dealt with quickly without much comment (or interest) from the peanut gallery.

"Next on the agenda," Calvin continued, "Bud Legaard is asking that we reconsider our eminent domain claim." Calvin looked out to the spectators. "Where is he?"

"He's not here." Lois clucked.

Andrea spoke up with some trepidation. "You did tell him that we wouldn't get to his item until 8:30?"

"It's nearly that." The wall clock read 8:11. "He goes around town saying that we're out to get him; but he can't be bothered to come to a meeting and make his case."

The council moved onto the next agenda item: the hospital tax initiative. A scowl grew on Jim's face as he watched Dennis Anderson gather his materials and approach the council. Jim disliked Dennis Anderson a great deal.

The hospital administrator presented his case with neatly-typed handouts containing graphs and charts and indisputable facts (which were, nonetheless disputed) about the need for a new one-percent local sales tax to help get the hospital out of the red. "This is not just a Kirby problem," Dennis read from his notes as if he were at a Congressional hearing instead of an elementary school located in a town too small to make it onto most maps, "Most every hospital in western North Dakota is running a deficit. When the oil workers came, the hospitals were inundated with new patients. Many of whom left the area without paying for services."

"You should have made 'em pay up front, then." Calvin suggested.

This statement pulled Dennis Anderson away from his prepared notes. He froze for a moment.

Ryan Peterson filled in the gap. "Saying what should have been done three years ago, doesn't change the situation that the hospital is in now, Mr. Mayor."

Recovered, Dennis spoke with some outrage in his usually controlled voice, "We're a hospital. We can't refuse to treat someone based on their inability to pay."

The look on the mayor's face said, "Why not?" but he had the good sense not to say it aloud.

Dennis continued with his prepared notes: "Similar sales taxes were approved years ago in Tioga and Williston."

"This isn't Tioga or Williston," Calvin interrupted again.

"We're not in the heart of this oil business like they are. St. Eustace never got the same kind of traffic those hospitals did." Calvin pointed an accusatory finger at Dennis. "Your hospital was hemorrhaging money long before the oil boom hit, and continues to today. This isn't an oil field problem. This is a problem of poor management. That's not going to change, no matter how much money you have coming in. I see no point in asking the people of Kirby to keep throwing good money after bad."

Dennis Anderson stood up. His eyes had the look of a madman's but his voice remained steady. "With all due respect mayor, that isn't your call to make. That's a decision that should be left up to the voters."

"They already made it." A similar sales tax initiative had been defeated in election two years prior.

"We have the right to present our case to them again. We have enough signatures to get on the ballot."

"You missed the deadline to get on November's ballot." Lois chimed in, helpful as always.

"Like hell I did." By this time Dennis' voice more closely matched his eyes. "Our next step is legal action."

Dennis Anderson tromped out of the room, brushing past Jim Rosdahl. As he passed, Dennis' arm touched Jim, and he felt a knot develop in his stomach that would remain with Jim until he went to bed that night.

In contrast, the mayor was able to brush off his encounter with Dennis as easily as brushing a clump of dirt from a pair of well-worn overalls. "Next item. Discussion on putting in a streetlight at Main and 2nd Avenue North."

Kirby was still a no-streetlight town. Earlier in the year, there had been a traffic accident at Main Street and 2nd Avenue North. It's a confusing three way intersection. Going north, Main Street ends in front of the county courthouse at 2nd Avenue North. Drivers on 2nd Avenue have a stop sign, but if you are driving up Main Street you can go right through, turning right or left onto 2nd. But you also have the option of making a U-turn and heading back south on Main. Don't worry if you don't understand it, out-of-towners rarely do.

In April, Mavis Eriksmoen had opted for the U-turn. The visitor, who was stopped on 2nd heading east, misinterpreted Mavis' wide U for a right hand turn and ended up T-boning her car – inasmuch as that is possible moving at less than 10 miles per hour. The next day, Mavis started a petition to get a streetlight put in at that intersection.

People in general don't like change. People in North Dakota have elevated not liking change to an art form. And so the "Save Our Streets" movement had trouble gaining traction. The campaign all but died in July when Mavis Eriksmoen moved to Grand Forks to live with her daughter and son-in-law. The "all but" being that the should-we-have-a-streetlight hoopla still made its way into discussions – and city council agendas from time to time.

After four minutes of discussion on the matter – and it becoming apparent that no one really wanted a streetlight – Calvin took in a deep breath. It's the breath he always took when preparing to adjourn the meeting.

"If there be no new-"

"Just one damn minute," came a voice from the hallway. Jim was a bit surprised to find himself being pushed aside by Bud Legaard as he entered the room. This was surprising as Bud Legaard was approximately 200 years old and not considered one of your more spritely bicentenarians.

"You're not taking my land." Bud informed Calvin Lystad and the rest of the city council.

In the height of the oil boom, a 15-plex apartment building had been constructed on the south end of town, an area that was incorporated but undeveloped. The city council decided the previous year to construct an access road from the apartments into town. To date, residents have to go south to the highway, then take the highway to the Farm-to-Market Road in order to go north back into town. The only place to put in an access road was over land that Bud Legaard owned. Bud didn't want to sell, so the city had declared eminent domain and taken the land. Construction on the football field length stripe of asphalt would begin in a few weeks, if the weather cooperated.

Bud owned property all over the region. And most of it, like the strip of land in question, went unused. The city had compensated Bud the fair market value for the land. And now the land would finally serve a useful purpose. The city council saw this as a "win-win."

Bud obviously felt otherwise. "Government swooping in and taking whatever they damn well please from a man who's worked all his life to have what he has, now."

Jim could see the validity of the city's decision, but wondered why they hadn't done it four years ago when the apartments were first built. Back then, there were actually people around to use the road. With the oil boom deflated, the apartments were less than half-full now.

"You're late, William. Meeting's over." Calvin referred to Bud by his given name. It irked Bud when people called him by the name his misguided parents had cursed him with at birth rather than the name he had come up with for himself. That is precisely why Calvin did it.

"I'm an old man." The comment didn't seem to be connected to anything; Bud was just saying what was on his mind.

"We can put you on the agenda again for next month."

"We're here already," Councilwoman Andrea Dhuyvetter said, "I don't mind hearing him out."

Ryan Peterson and even Jon Knutson agreed with Andrea. Calvin was outnumbered. But then he saw his trump card.

"Lois has already packed up her stuff," he said. The meeting was adjourned with no other objection from the council members.

Bud Legaard hadn't run out of objections, however. "I'll

sue you for everything you got, Cal. Sue your entire family. Your wife, your brothers, your mother. Think you're so high and mighty. You're not a damn thing. I know where you come from." The threat of legal action, twice in one city council meeting. *That will make for a good story*, Jim thought.

"Go home, William."

"Kirby will be a lot better off when you're lying in the cold, wet ground, Calvin Lystad."

This was the second time today someone had wished for the death of the mayor within earshot of Jim. *An even better story*, he thought. *Not suitable for The Crier, though.*

That's a tale someone else would have to tell.

5

"He said, 'I'll sue you, Cal?'" Betty Lindstrom asked for clarification.

"'Cal. Like they were fishing buddies," Ardis Knudsvig confirmed, "Then he went on to say he would sue Calvin's wife, his brothers, and his mother."

The day after the city council meeting, the news mill was in full swing over at the Clark County Senior Citizen Center. A group of elderly widows gathered to watch Edith Andrist's apple pie making demonstration: over the course of which Edith had been advised by her "students" that if you slice the apples instead of just cutting them into wedges the pie would be more tender; if you start the oven at a higher temperature and then lower it the crust would brown better; and you could use oleo instead of butter for the crust and it turns out just fine, no matter what Louise's daughter-in-law said to the contrary.

After Edith's exhausting demonstration, the ladies sat at the bridge table to eat the fruits of her labor and to discuss the latest in the Calvin Lystad saga.

"His mother? Why Mabel's been dead for decades." Louise Granrud said. "Edith, this crust is so flaky, now" she added, even though she felt it was a little too dry.

All the other widows agreed.

Always on the search for clarity, Betty Lindstrom turned to Gladys Rosdahl. "What do you think that meant?"

"Ramblings of a crazy fool," Gladys Rosdahl asserted.

"Uff da," chimed in Margaret Stromstad, who wasn't a widow yet but the other ladies tried to not make her feel like an outcast. "I'm afraid Bud may be getting senile. I was out with the dog last week and I ran into him. We got to talking, ya know. He was walking home because he had gone downtown and then forgotten where he parked his car. So sad, ya know."

"But he didn't mention Calvin's father? Does that mean something?" Betty wanted to know. "Ardis, are you sure that's what Bud said?"

"That's what Ardis told me. And her boy Jon is on the council now, you know, so I suppose he would know what Bud said."

Gladys, who had also been at the meeting confirmed this.

Ardis Knudsvig went on to tell Edith, "That pie was so good" - it was not - "and your crust! I always manage to burn mine" - she did not - "I'm going to have to try adding that hint of nutmeg" - she would not.

"Would you like another slice?" Edith Andrist asked. "There's still plenty more."

"Oh no, I don't want to ruin my dinner."

The other widows also did not wish to ruin their respective dinners.

- - - -

Two weeks later, at the Kirby Auto Parts, the conflict between the mayor and the hospital administrator was the more compelling story. Lars Whalon, owner and proprietor, stood behind his counter addressing the men seated on the bar stools that Lars had purchased for just such occasions.

"Ya, the hospital has hired a lawyer from over there in Bismarck to help 'em, you know." Lars repeated the information he had given these gentlemen on the previous day.

"Bismarck, you say?" Arnie Lund said as he had yesterday, and sipped his coffee. His stool mate, Verner Svangstu read his newspaper, *The Minot Daily News* (since *The Kirby Crier* would not come out for two more days.)

"Oh ya, got him on what's called 'retainer,'" Lars shared this new information.

"What's that?" Arnie asked knowing full well what a retainer was – but this was Lars' court, not his.

"It means he don't get paid until the hospital gets what they want," Verner said, never looking up from his paper.

"Ya, I don't think it means that," Arnie said.

"All I know," said Lars, "is that the hospital is suing the city and I just want to know what that means for us come tax time."

"Ya," came Arnie.

"Also, that Bismarck lawyer ain't no he. He's a her."

"Ya?" from Arnie.

"Ya?" from Verner.

"Yip. From what I hear, she's a real pretty thing but a real" and here Lars dropped his voice "b word."

"Oh, I bet she is." Arnie chuckled. "I would never mess with Dennis Anderson. He seems all cool and proper, but he does not like it when he don't get his way."

At this point, Lars' assistant Lee Johnson who had been sweeping in the back, made an appearance. At 27, Lee was a downright infant next to Lars, Arnie and Verner. "I went pheasant hunting with Dennis once. He bagged his limit and bagged my limit, then we called it a day. I never even got a shot off."

The room fell into a polite silence as Lee reflected and the other men tried to figure out what the hell this had to do with anything.

Lee Johnson continued, "Think maybe he was traumatized by a pheasant as a kid or something?"

Without his eyes ever leaving his newspaper, Verner got the conversation back on track. "I don't want any of this hospital sales tax nonsense."

Lars said, "Even so, Dennis has the right to have it put to a vote."

"It was put to a vote. The whole town voted against it. What's changed in a year?"

"They've done put a lot of ads in *The Crier* to drum up support."

"Ya, spending a bunch of money they claim they don't have."

"Still, it might have done the trick. A lot of people are in favor of it now. But Cal is still against it, so there's no way he's letting it go to a vote."

Lars and Verner fell silent. They were at odds on this one. Arnie, ever the consensus builder, said, "If Dennis is going in with guns blazing, next month's council meeting should be quite a spectacle."

"Ya."

"Ya."

"Guns, heh." The men turned to Lee, who was off in his own little world. Lee noticed the men noticing him. "Calvin Lystad should just thank his lucky stars he's not a pheasant."

– – – –

At Jen's Yarn Barn the following week, the conversations about Calvin Lystad focused on his personal life.

"Guess who I saw Calvin Lystad having lunch with, on my way over here?" *Crier* employee Layla Hedahl asked her Aunt Marsha.

"No!"

Layla nodded.

Marsha was aghast. "Having lunch together? They're not even trying to hide it anymore."

"Saw them walk right into the Burger Shack together."

"Burger Shack. Only the best for Cal Lystad. And right on Main Street where everyone can see them."

Marsha held a certain level of contempt for the Burger Shack. When Mickey Kilroy had moved to Kirby from the East Coast 12 years ago, he opened a restaurant called the Burger Barn. Marsha felt the name detracted from her store – Jen's

Yarn Barn – which had been around since the 70s. After some discussion, Mickey agreed to change the Burger Barn to the Burger Shack; though he still contended that the name Jen's Yarn Barn made no sense whatsoever. Indeed, Jen's Yarn Barn – which Marsha Hedahl had purchased in 1994 – had not belonged to anyone named Jen in some time, and had stopped selling yarn even before that. The one-time craft supply store had morphed into a women's apparel and home decor shop when the J. C. Penney closed down. Though entirely inappropriate, the name Jen's Yarn Barn was never changed because people in Kirby don't particularly like change. Also there were more important matters in life to concern themselves with.

"To think, I used to like that Abby Quicke." Marsha shook her head. "She sure had me fooled. Always smiling and laughing and happy. She's from New England, you know. Poor Hazel."

"Abby's lived here for at least a decade." Layla felt the need to play devil's advocate a bit.

"Decade. Oh, that's nothing."

"They could be just friends."

"Oh, you sweet, naïve thing. Let me tell you something." Aunt Marsha laid it out for *The Crier's* layout manager. "Calvin Lystad may be in his sixties, but he acts like a man in his fifties. And men in their fifties are idiots." Marsha paused to allow Layla to speak, but there was no arguing with that logic, so Marsha continued. "They finally realize that they have more life behind them then ahead of them. So they suddenly have to find anything to make them feel young again. First, they thrust off the shackles of their marriage and they start gallivanting with some new chippy."

"Isn't Abby about the same age as Hazel?"

"Don't matter. She's new to him. At first he's ashamed – as he should be – and hides the affair. But then, he decides it's not enough to feel young again. He wants other people to know that he's the kind of guy who can still turn a head. So he starts parading her around, ya know. That's what Cal's doing now."

"What does he do after that?" Abby asked.

"If he's smart, he'll remember that he's married to a woman who's a few yards short of an acre, and end the affair before his wife stabs him through the heart with a kitchen knife."

6

October 12. Wednesday evening. Weeks earlier, the geese predicted an early winter. They had been right on the mark. The meteorologist out of Minot forcast a moderate to severe winter storm overnight for the entire northwestern part of the state. What North Dakotans call a "winter storm" the rest of the world calls a "blizzard" (and what a certain sheriff's deputy who was used to Tucson winters would come to call "Snowmageddon"). In Wildrose, North Dakota, Donna Fulstrom settled into the den to wait out the storm with a blanket, a cup of hot cocoa, and a book by Danielle Steele. In Bowbells, Carl Ingwaldson double checked that his snowplow was in good working order – he would need it in the morning. Outside of Tioga, Brandon DiCuomo hoped that the sheets of plywood he put up around the base of the tiny RV that was serving as his home would keep it warm enough so that he could go on to live another day on the oil derrick.

By contrast, in Kirby folks were preparing to go out. The city council was meeting tonight. As a general rule, council meetings were not well attended, but this one was slated to be an eventful one. Over a hundred people – almost ten percent of the population– had made plans to be there. Some wanted to show their support for Dennis Anderson and the hospital. A few wished to applaud the council's decision on the matter. Some had heard rumors that Hazel Lystad would show up and make a scene, and they wanted to see it. Others came because they knew that Bud Legaard would show up and make a scene. At least one person – Eunice Nielsen – wanted to make sure they weren't going to put in a streetlight. These people were bound and determined: they were going to that city council meeting come hell or eight to twelve inches of snow with winds gusting up to 40 miles an hour.

As ever, the meeting was slated for 7:30 in the evening. As never, the meeting was being held at the L&C Movie Theater, which was next door to *The Crier*. In the last four weeks, the speculation about the upcoming meeting was growing into the stuff of legend. The council members soon realized that there was no way the Kathleen Rosdahl Room would be large enough to hold all of the folks that planned to attend. In an uncharacteristic show of strength, the city council insisted – over city clerk Lois Pedersen's objections – that the venue for the next meeting be moved to the theater.

Folks started arriving at the Lewis & Clark Movie Theater a little before 7 to ensure that they got a good seat. Eunice Nielsen arrived at 7 p.m. on the dot. . . at the elementary school rather than the theater. Seeing no one around, she went home and prayed they wouldn't put in that traffic light.

Snow had been falling steadily but slowly for an hour. The strong wind caused the snow on the ground to dance along the sidewalk rather than stick to one spot. By 7:20, when Jim Rosdahl arrived, the rate of snowfall had picked up considerably, and the accumulation on the ground started behaving itself.

"Your first snowstorm?" Jim asked Deputy Aidan Gray when he saw him in the lobby.

"This is impossible. It's not even Halloween yet." his friend marveled.

"Geese don't lie."

"What?"

"Nothing."

"You want anything?" Aidan was fourth in line to get snacks. L&C manager Mel Throntveit had agreed to let the city council meet in the single-screen movie theater on the condition that he could open up the concession stand and make a few bucks. "You don't see a lot of government meetings where they sell popcorn."

"Dinner and a show," Jim said with a smile. "I'll meet you

in there."

Seats were filling up quickly inside the theater. Jim scoped out two spots near the back, but decided not to sit down. Instead, he pulled a small notepad out of his back pocket and headed down the aisle. Andrea Dhuyvetter, Jon Knutson and Ryan Peterson were milling about the tables that had been set up in front of the movie screen.

"Quite a crowd tonight," Jim addressed Ryan, who was wringing his hands. Nerves, probably.

"People love to watch a train wreck." The polished, rehearsed councilman seemed uncomfortable in his own skin tonight. Ryan saw the notepad in Jim's hand, "off the record."

Jim smiled but didn't speak.

"Where's your reporter?"

"Brian drove to Minot this morning to pick Judith's mother up from the airport. Didn't want to drive back tonight with the storm." This was an entirely legitimate excuse, but it still irked Jim. With Brian Jacobson, it was always something.

"Our mayor's not in Minot is he?" Jim looked around to confirm that Calvin Lystad was nowhere to be seen.

"I don't know where he is, Jim. Maybe he wised up and decided to leave town."

The fact that Ryan Peterson despised Calvin Lystad was not common knowledge. Jim knew it; he and Ryan were friends. Like many politicians, Ryan was a good actor. He might argue with Calvin on policy, but he never showed a personal distaste for the mayor in public. In private was another matter. In Ryan's eyes, Calvin Lystad was a supercilious blowhard who used politics for personal gain. Ryan considered his mayor a barely literate ape who couldn't be trusted with the town's money and resources. Jim thought some of that bluster may just be Ryan's bruised ego from having lost the mayoral election to Calvin the previous year.

"Dennis Anderson isn't here yet," Jim realized.

"Bud Legaard hasn't shown up either. Though he's always

late."

"Maybe they're in a back room somewhere, slugging it out with the mayor." Jim said.

Ryan smiled at this. "I hope they beat the *mmhnm* out of him." Ryan glanced at Jim's notepad once more. "Allegedly."

"Perhaps the storm has scared them off," Andrea offered. It was a plausible, if unconvincing, possibility.

"It's almost time for the meeting to start," Jim observed. "What happens if Calvin doesn't show up?"

"Calvin Lystad is not the city council. We'll give him 15 minutes and then we'll start without him."

And that's exactly what they did. The meeting was called to order. People took their seats, munching on popcorn and Charleston Chews. Ryan was selected to serve as Chairman *ex officio*. Lois Pedersen objected to beginning the meeting without the mayor but Jon pointed out that she was not a member of the council and therefore did not have a say. Without Calvin there to back her up, Lois seemed to deflate.

The first item on the agenda was the new daycare. To everyone's puzzlement, Val Bakke – who ran the daycare and was leading the charge in getting the larger facility built – was nowhere to be seen. Neither was her sheriff husband, Tor Bakke, for that matter. Denise Bjorgen, who also worked at the daycare, was put on the spot. Denise stumbled through what she knew about the progress of the project, which wasn't much.

Claire Glasoe stood up and tried to fill in the gaps in Denise's knowledge. Claire did not work for or use the daycare, but she was married to Val's brother Gordy, and as such believed that she had sufficient knowledge to talk about the daycare.

Allan Borreson – who had come to snap a few pictures for *The Crier* – set down his camera and stood up to do the one thing he enjoyed more than anything else in life: correcting other people. "Claire, that state grant was for $12,000, not $20,000." Then Allan turned toward the council to do his second favorite thing in life: accusing other people. "What I want to know is, what is the council doing with all that money from the lodging tax? Why can't that go to build the daycare?"

When oil had come to town, every hotel room in town was filled up with men and women (mostly men) who couldn't find an apartment, RV or man camp to live in. To capitalize on their misfortune, the city had added a lodging tax. Three years later, the city still wasn't sure what to do with the windfall.

"Well Allan," Ryan Peterson stumbled to find his words. "I don't know that we've gotten that far into the process yet. We are assessing-" Ryan's words broke off as he looked past Allan to the back of the theater. He said, in a tone that he hoped sounded like good-natured ribbing, "Glad you could finally join us."

The crowd turned in their seats to see Calvin Lystad standing at the entrance. He's drunk, Jim thought as he watched Calvin's body sway. But the look on Calvin's face didn't indicate inebriation, but panic. That's when Jim noticed the thing which should have been most obvious: a large red stain on the front of his shirt.

Ryan continued, "Did your forget how to get around in all this snow." The question mark was dropped from Ryan's tone as Calvin's condition finally registered in his mind. Ryan stood. "Mayor? Cal?"

Calvin Lystad collapsed onto the floor, rolled six feet down the slanted movie aisle, and ended up on his back. Mickey Kilroy, owner of the Burger Shack and volunteer ambulance driver, was the first to reach Calvin.

He had already lost consciousness.

7

In the movies when tragedy strikes, things fall apart. People form camps. They turn on each other. They get into arguments at the drop of a hat. This is a storytelling technique called "raising the stakes."

In real life, though, tragedy often unifies people. Strangers work together. Enemies momentarily put away petty differences to deal with a real problem. A few leaders emerge and everyone else stays the hell out of their way.

When Calvin Lystad collapsed in the L&C Movie Theater, Mickey Kilroy, Deputy Aidan Gray, Councilwoman Andrea Dhuyvetter and Jim Rosdahl rushed to his side. Everyone else got out of their way.

Mickey, a certified EMT, began administering CPR.

"Is he shot?" Andrea asked.

Mickey breathed into Calvin, then began pressing on his chest.

"Stabbed. Looks like," Jim said. He turned to Aidan. "Call the ambulance?"

Andrea – who in addition to being on the city council was the only female volunteer emergency responder in the county – shook her head. "We're all here. I could send someone to get it, but I think it would be quicker to take him in someone's car."

"I have my cruiser," Aidan said.

Eye contact and a short nod indicated that they were in agreement. Jim and Aidan lifted Calvin as carefully as they could. Mickey fell back against the wall of the Theater, exhausted. Andrea ran ahead to catch the door.

In the lobby, Aidan said, "We need to get some officers

down here. This is a crime scene."

"I'm on it." Andrea remained in the lobby to make the call as the two men went outside. The snowfall had grown in intensity. Heavy winds caused it to come in almost horizontally. The five inches that had already accumulated on the ground shifted like sand dunes.

Jim and Aidan gingerly laid Calvin in the back seat of Aidan's cruiser, losing hope by the second. When Jim reached for the passenger door, Aidan said, "Stay here."

"What do you need?"

"Make sure everybody says put. No one can leave until the sheriff's had a chance to interview them."

Jim nodded. He heard the car's siren come to life as he ran back to the theater.

8

When Sheriff Tor Bakke arrived at the theater he told everyone to go home. "We'll contact you if we need you."

The crowd moved out. People opted to exit from the south aisle, avoiding the spot on the north aisle where Calvin had collapsed. Jim went in the opposite direction toward the screen, where the sheriff, the city clerk and the council members were congregated.

"How's the mayor?" Lois asked Jim. She was on the verge of tears.

"I haven't heard yet. He'll be at the hospital now."

"They're not equipped for this kind of thing. We need to get him airlifted to Minot."

"The helicopter couldn't make it in this storm," Tor said.

Even without a storm, Jim thought, *that chopper would have to come from Minot first; there was no way Calvin had that kind of time.* Jim left this reality unsaid. "Our people know what they're doing." He placed a hand on Lois' shoulder. He wanted to offer comfort, but he didn't know how. He and Lois were not friends. And, like most good Norwegians, Jim wasn't the touchy-feely sort. Jim suddenly wished that Claudette were here. His wife was much better at the emotional stuff.

Lois offered Jim something that resembled a smile and joined the mass exodus. Jim turned towards the sheriff.

"Ya, I got nothing to say right now, Jim." Tor said before Jim got out word one. "Once I have some idea what's happened, I'll call you. Now go home, now."

"Deputy Gray seemed to think you'd want to talk to some of these people." Jim said.

"Gray." Tor gave a sigh which indicated he had more to say

about his deputy, but he didn't say it. What he did say, in a strained rather than harsh tone was, "Jim. Go home. I'll call you when I have some handle on this."

Jim left the theater through the emergency exit that let out into the alley. He tromped through the heavy snow that was still accumulating. He had promised his mother that he would fill her in on the events of the evening after the council meeting. Gladys Rosdahl was good at hiding her emotions – she was an even better Norwegian than her son – but Jim could tell that she had been anxious about this meeting. Jim's mother had no appetite for conflict and confrontation and this meeting was slated to be the blow up of the decade in Kirby. Gladys wanted no part in any of it. . . though she still wanted to hear what happened.

Even if the promise of conflict hadn't kept her away, the venue would have. Gladys Rosdahl lived across the alley from the L&C Movie Theater, but she had never stepped inside it. Most churchgoing folk in Western North Dakota are Lutherans, with the occasional Catholic thrown in for flavor. But the Bakke family (that Gladys was born into) and the Rosdahl family (which she married into) had attended the Assembly of God church since 1934 – the year an AG Tent Revival came through Kirby and the Bakkes and the Rosdahls and a few assorted others gave their hearts to Jesus. During Gladys's formative years, you couldn't love both Jesus and Gary Cooper, so movies were out. Even though very few people still felt that way, Gladys Bakke Rosdahl was old school. In her 82 years on earth, she had never been inside a movie theater.

Jim opened the front door to his mother's house. No need to use a key, she never locked her doors. (She also always kept the keys in the ignition of her car.)

Jim found his mother in the kitchen mopping the floor. Gladys cleaned when she was anxious. Jim thought, *I should have had her wait over at my place; the dishes are really stacking up since Claudette went to Bismarck.*

Gladys stopped mopping and looked up at her son. "Well," she asked, "how did it go?"

Jim's phone beeped. "The mayor collapsed at the theater."

"He what?"

Jim looked at the text message he had just received from Aidan. "Calvin Lystad is dead."

Gladys plated up a few of the chocolate peanut butter oatmeal bars that she had made that afternoon. She and Jim sat in silence at the breakfast table in the kitchen. Neither had an appetite, but they ate the bars – you don't make bars and then not eat them.

In the silence, Jim thought about who would want to kill Calvin Lystad. He could think of a few dozen people who were angry with Calvin – a few you'd go as far as to say, hated the man – but Jim couldn't wrap his mind around the thought that anyone would go so far as to murder him. This wasn't Chicago or Detroit. Hell, this wasn't even Bismarck. This was Kirby, North Dakota. A little farming community, where you knew everybody and everybody knew you. And you liked everybody; even the people that you hated.

Gladys could not bear the silence any longer. She also couldn't bear to talk about the real news of the evening. "I talked to Heike today," she said. Heike Odegaard worked at the Kirby Kuttery Salon.

"Ya," Jim said. "I see it. Your hair looks nice."

Gladys let out a dismissive sigh. "I didn't get it done. She called me from Arizona." Harlan and Heike Odegaard belonged to a growing breed of animals called "snowbirds" who had the time and money to spend summers at their real home and winters at a second home located closer to the equator. There were more than a few snowbirds residing in Kirby. The Odegaards. The Stromstads. Arnie Lund. Even Kirby's mayor was. . . or rather, had been. . . a snowbird.

"It's a little early in the year, isn't it?" Jim asked.

Gladys looked out the window at the Snowmageddon outside. "Maybe not."

"Ya."

"Bud Legaard left yesterday, I think."

"Must be why he wasn't there tonight. Arizona?"

"Florida."

"I thought it was Arizona." Jim took the empty dishes over to the sink and began to wash them. "Doesn't make much sense that he would go there now. What with the city trying to take his land."

After Jim washed the dishes in silence they went into the living room and settled down to watch the last twenty minutes of an episode of *Dr. Quinn, Medicine Woman* that Gladys had already seen at least a dozen times. It was during the good doctor's impassioned speech to the shop owner that it wasn't the color of his skin that made a man a savage, Jim received a phone call.

"Can you come to the station? Right now" Aidan's voice was low and troubled.

"Could I come over in the morning to make my statement?"

"We've made an arrest in the mayor's case."

"Who?"

Aidan ignored the question. "How soon can you get here? I need someone who's good at asking the right questions."

"You want me to interrogate a prisoner?" Jim asked with just a twinge of levity in case this turned out to be a joke. Gladys turned off the television and observed her son with curiosity.

Aidan sighed. "Just get down here."

9

Earlier in the day, Jim had left his car at his mother's house, but now there was too much snow on the roads to drive. He walked the quarter of a mile to the Sheriff's Office, tromping through eight inches of snow while more continued to fall. The temperature was venturing into negative numbers, but the wind had died down, which made the walk bearable. In North Dakota, a day without wind is a good day. Even if you can't feel your toes.

Aidan's words ran through Jim's mind. "I need someone who's good at asking the right questions." Jim asked questions for a living, but asking the Kirby Chamber of Commerce president what kind of turnout they expected for the bingo night fundraiser was a lot different than shaking down a murder suspect for information. Surely, this was a job better suited to the law enforcement officers – even if none of them had ever been on a murder case before.

Jim arrived at the station. Outwardly, things seemed at peace: the sheriff in his office with the door open, Aidan at his desk and Deputy Tim Aarons sitting at the desk furthest from Aidan's. The room was silent.

Too silent, Jim felt. It appeared that the three men were going out of their way to not look at each other. There was a heaviness in the air like a married couple's house after a knockdown, drag out fight.

Aidan did not rise when he saw Jim. He gave a slight smile, but he said nothing and made no movements.

"What the hell are you doing here, cousin?" came a bellow from the sheriff's office. Tor Bakke jumped out of his chair – no small feat for a short man tipping the scale at 300 pounds

– and came barreling toward Jim.

"I don't really know."

"Your presence here is a disruption, and not-"

"I asked him to come," Aidan interrupted.

Tor turned to his deputy. His mouth was agape but words escaped him.

"The press has a right to know when we've made an arrest," Aidan continued.

"Don't give me any freedom of the press bull. This isn't the press; this is Jim. Son of farmers."

Jim resisted the urge to correct Tor – only his mother's side of the family were farmers – and instead asked, "Have you made an arrest already?"

"I'm not going to answer that, cousin."

Aidan answered for him. "He's a 27-year-old Hispanic male. Tomás Escobar." Aidan gave the name the correct Spanish pronunciation: Toe-Moss. "He didn't do it, Jim."

"That's enough, deputy." Tor shouted. "Sit your ass down." Aidan considered his options and then did as he was commanded.

"Who is this guy, sheriff?"

"This Tom Estesban lives over at Kirby Farms" – an RV community on the northwestern edge of town – "and claims to work for Trident Oil. We're still working to verify that." From where Jim was standing, it didn't seem like anyone was working to verify anything.

"He admit that he did it?" Jim asked.

"Yes, Jim. The criminals always admit to their crimes."

"How did you find this guy?"

At this question, Tim stood up. Tim Aarons was the only Jewish resident of Kirby. Of Clark County. The 31 year old's most dominant facial features were a stereotypical Semitic nose and a thick, dark unibrow. His six-foot-four frame was carrying at least 100 pounds too many. Despite all of this, Tim still gave off a Barney Fife vibe.

"I received a call at 8:09 this evening of a disturbance at Maddy's Bar on Main and Central." *Everyone here knows where Maddy's is, Deputy Fife,* Jim thought. "I arrived to find three men physically restraining one Thomas Ezz-ca-bar. The proprietor reports that Mr. Ezz-ca-bar had been drinking steadily since 11 this morning. At approximately 6:30, he and another bar patron got into a heated argument. At which point, Thomas left the bar. He returned around 8:00 pm with a gun. He then proceeded to stand outside in the snowstorm, shouting obscenities and firing a weapon into the air."

"That's it?" Jim asked. "What am I missing?"

Tor came up behind Jim and placed his hand on Jim's shoulder. "Why don't you head home? I promise I will call you in the morning about where we are in the investigation."

"Of course," Jim said. Tor took his hand off Jim's shoulder and relaxed noticeably. "Could we just talk privately for a minute first?"

They exchanged a look. Jim's smile was friendly, but his eyes were pure steel. "Sure, cuz."

They went into the sheriff's office. Tor closed the door behind him, which — like so many things tonight — was a rare occurrence. The sheriff offered Jim a seat which he declined. He then sat at his desk.

Only moments ago, Jim had arrived wondering why he would be needed to talk to a suspect. Now he realized that there was someone else Aidan wanted him to interrogate.

"Your friend Deputy Gray is eager," Tor began. "A little bit of eagerness is good in this job. But too much eagerness is a liability. Gray is going to be the death of me, cousin."

Tor called Jim cousin from time to time. Tor Bakke's grandfather Adam and Jim's mother had been cousins. To Jim's mind, this made him and Tor fourth cousins completely removed.

"You've arrested the wrong man." Jim protested, his voice louder than usual. He was ready for a fight.

Tor did not play along. He sounded exhausted. "My birthday was last week."

"Congratulations," Jim huffed. "This man had a gun. If he was looking to kill Calvin, wouldn't he have just shot him? And suppose he did stab him, why would he start shooting his gun into the air to draw attention to himself?"

"I turned 47."

The sheriff's statements were throwing Jim off his game. He sat down.

"I look young for my age, they tell me."

Tor was short, heavy, and his blonde hair had receded halfway up his head – he looked old. "Sure," Jim agreed.

"So to look at me, you might not realize that I was not, in fact, born yesterday, cousin."

"You know he didn't do it?" Jim was surprised.

"I can't rule it out completely yet," the sheriff said, "but it seems unlikely."

"Why do you have him under arrest?"

"He's the only thing I've got right now, Jim." Tor rested his heavy head into the cup of his right hand. "People need us to arrest someone. It will make them feel safer."

"But if this man didn't-"

Tor regained some of his energy. "The last time I checked, Jim, firing an unregistered weapon into the air was still against the law. I'll defer to your legal expertise on that one."

Jim ignored the sarcasm. "How is the investigation going?"

Tor let out an unhappy laugh. "What investigation? I've got my other two guys down at the theater securing the scene. We've called in reinforcements. That's what I know to do." Before Jim could jump on that, Tor continued. "This has never happened before, cuz. Clark County Sheriff's Office is a little short on homicide detectives."

Something clicked in Jim's mind. "Is that why Aidan is so up in arms?"

Distractedly, Tor twirled a pen in his hand. "He's got a

bee in his bonnet about dismissing everyone at the theater. Thinks I botched this thing from the start. Didn't talk to witnesses. Let them trample through the scene, destroying evidence." Tor slammed the pen onto the desk. "I couldn't just keep a hundred people locked up all night with a blizzard outside. And all those 'witnesses' saw exactly the same thing: an already stabbed Calvin Lystad stumbling into the theater and dying."

Jim hated to admit it, but he could see Tor's point. Still his decisions seemed a little short-sighted. Perhaps Calvin had said something when he first came in that folks near the back heard. These folks wouldn't necessarily come to the sheriff of their own accord. "It probably wasn't important," those people were thinking at this moment, "And I don't want to make a fuss."

But Jim supposed if that had happened, the word would get around town eventually. It always did. There are no secrets in a small town.

"Gray is going to be a constant thorn in my side until we 'nab the perp.' What do I do?"

"He wants an investigation. Let him have it."

Tor considered this. "It would get him out of my hair. But none of my guys want to work with him, Jim. He's too eager. And he thinks we're all a bunch of backwoods yokels who can't find their asses with a map." *Most of the officers of Clark County have quite ample asses,* Jim thought, *they would be hard to miss.*

"Why does he need a partner?"

Tor starting talking before all of the words had left Jim's mouth. "I'm not sending that kid out half-cocked. His eagerness is going to cause him to make mistakes. And he doesn't know this town. These people. He needs a babysitter."

"I'll do it." Jim blurted out the words before his brain had signed off on them.

"What?"

"I know Kirby. I know how to conduct an interview. I can keep Aidan under control." Jim's brain had caught up now and was saying, "What are you doing?"

Jim's line about keeping his new friend under control like he was a frisky dog was the height of ridiculousness, but it struck a chord with Tor. His silence indicated that he was thinking about it. After a few moments he looked up at Jim, "I couldn't deputize you."

"Like hell you couldn't," Jim wanted to say. What he said was: "That's not necessary. I'll be a consultant."

"Unpaid." Tor considered, then shook his head. "Tempting. But probably not the greatest idea."

"Think of it this way, cousin." Jim could feel his skin crawling at the word. "You'll not only get this deputy off your back, you'll get that pesky reporter out of your hair."

Tor considered a few more moments.

"You don't touch anything," he said finally. Jim nodded in agreement. "Anything. You're there to babysit. You can ask questions and make observations. Nothing else. And you don't do anything without Deputy Gray with you."

Jim assented.

"And I get to approve any stories about this case before they go to print."

In its entire 90-plus years in existence, *The Kirby Crier* had a strict policy of no-editorial interference. Not in politics, not in police work, not even in fluff community news, were the parties involved ever allowed to even see the stories beforehand. Approval of a news story was beyond the pale. A complete and utter deal breaker.

"Deal," Jim said, extending his hand. The men shook on it.

"I'll tell you. I wish it were this Tom Estesbar." Tor got a faraway look in his eyes. "An outsider. I can't bear the thought of it being someone from here."

For once, Jim knew exactly how Tor Bakke felt.

10

Sheriff Tor Bakke informed Deputy Aidan Gray that he would be in charge of Kirby's investigative efforts on the Calvin Lystad murder case; Aidan smiled. Tor then told him that Jim would assisting him; Aidan laughed out of reflex.

A few residual chuckles escaped Aidan as he and Jim made their way down the hallway to the holding cell. "My older sister used to get three bucks an hour to watch me. I hope you're getting at least that."

"Funny." Jim said. "See if you can keep a straight face through this interrogation."

"Interrogation?" Aidan smiled. "Look at you, all *Law & Order*. This guy didn't do anything. He doesn't know anything. His only crime is being born Mexican."

Jim didn't appreciate his friend's implication, that everyone in the department – and by extension, everyone in the town – were a bunch of racists. Jim didn't appreciate being called a racist; even if he wasn't actually being called one.

Places like North Dakota have a reputation for being homogenous, but nothing could be further from the truth. A visitor to this great state might see only a sea of white faces. In truth, North Dakota is as diverse as they come. You've got your Norwegians, your Danes, your Swedes, your Finns, and even some Icelanders thrown in for color. But that's not all, there are plenty more people in North Dakota who aren't of Scandinavian decent at all. You've got your Belgians and your Germans and your Russians. There might even be some Englishmen lurking about here and there.

Of course, when the oil boom hit, diversity ramped up a notch. Plenty of outsiders came flooding into the state to work – black men, Latino men, white men. Some moved to the Bak-

ken, but most just looked at North Dakota as their job site.
They would work three weeks in a row and then fly home to
Albuquerque or Atlanta or Abilene to spend a week with their
families before flying back to work. Many Kirbyites were wary
of the oil men, not because they were black or Hispanic, but
because they were tourists. When the boom went bust, these
men drained out as quickly as they had flooded in.

"Not to discount your 'He's Mexican' theory," Jim said,
"but this man was also carrying an unlicensed weapon. And
firing that weapon. And making threats to someone."

They reached the end of the hall. The prisoner sat on a
cot in a tiny cell. The only cell they had. Clark County didn't
have a jail proper, just a place to hold folks until they could be
transported to the prison in Williams County to the south.

"Tomás Escobar," Aidan said, as he grabbed two chairs and
moved them near the outside of the cell.

"I didn't mean to do it. I swear."

Jim had expected the man to have a thick accent and speak
in broken English. But aside from being panicky and intox-
icated, Tomás spoke perfectly clear English. Jim thought,
Maybe I am racist.

"What didn't you mean to do, Tomás?" Aidan asked.

Tomás buried his face into his hands. He started shaking.
Jim surmised that Mr. Ezz-co-bar had begun to cry. Tomás
tried several times to speak, but the words would not come.

"I need you to speak to me, Tomás."

The prisoner raised his head and tried to get his breathing
under control. Tomás rubbed his hands across his face to wipe
away the tears that covered it.

"I was just shooting into the air. I didn't mean to hit anyone. It was an accident. You have to believe me."

Aidan and Jim exchanged a confused look.

"Who did you shoot, Tomás?" Aidan asked.

"They told me I killed your mayor. Oh God." Tomás started
sobbing again. He said something after this, but neither of the

men could make it out. He might not have been speaking English at this point.

Aidan gave Tomás a few moments to compose himself, before continuing. "Tell us what happened."

"I was drinking. Been there most of the day." There, being Maddy's Bar. "This ass Ran-" Tomás cut himself off before he began naming names. He continued, "this other guy comes in and starts picking a fight with me."

Aidan must not have thought the other man's name was relevant, because he simply told Tomás to go on.

"He's bigger than me and I've had a few too many – but I wasn't drunk! – so he's able to bounce me out. So I scream 'I'll be back.' I go to my place, grab the gun and come back. I stand outside the bar swinging the gun and shouting for this guy to come outside. I fire a couple of shots into the air. To scare him. That's all. One of them shots must be what came down and hit your mayor. I didn't mean to do it."

Jim who had been silent to this point, decided to ease this guy's mind. "The mayor wasn't -" Aidan set his hand on Jim's shoulder. Jim instinctively knew that this was a request to stop talking.

"You see the mayor get hit?" Aidan asked.

"No, but I saw him right before. Outside the bar. Before I started firing."

"How do you know it was the mayor?"

"Must've been. He was the only other guy out there."

"What did he look like?"

"Like every other guy out here. White. Old."

Maybe I'm not the only one who's racist, Jim thought.

"I need more than that, Tomás," Aidan spoke with intensity. "A description. Your freedom is on the line here." Many times on television, Jim had seen the old good cop/bad cop routine. He decided that his friend made an excellent "bad cop." He wasn't sure how to play "good cop" so he continued in his role of "silent not a cop."

"I only saw him from the back. And he was like 300 feet down the street." Tomás pleaded. About a block separates Maddy's Bar from the L&C Movie Theater on Main Street. *His story checks out*, Jim thought in his TV-detective-influenced mind.

Aidan said in a mock southern accent, "That's some pretty keen perception' in the middle of a blizzard by a guy who's raving mad and drunk off his ass."

"I was not drunk." Here Tomás stood up for the first time. Aidan motioned for Tomás to sit back down. He did.

"I can see you're scared, Tomás. You're trying to say the right things, the words that will make you seem innocent; but you're not doing yourself any favors by making up stories."

Tomás stood up again. "No, I swear it's the truth," he insisted. "I was shouting and looking up and down the street. And I saw this guy walking, even through the snow I could see him. He was down by the grocery store, kind of swaying. Like a drunk. I remember thinking, *What kind of idiot would be outside in all this snow and sh-*." Tomás laughed a bit at this. "Too stupid to realize that I was doing the same damn thing."

More like too drunk, Jim thought. Tomás took a deep breath and sat back on his cot.

"You didn't see him again?" Aidan asked.

"No, he was walking away from the bar."

Jim perked up. "Walking away from you?" Jim pulled his chair closer. "Thomas, are you sure this man you saw was by the grocery store?"

"Yeah."

Like the movie theater, the grocery store was also located on Main Street and was also a block away from Maddy's Bar. But in the opposite direction.

Aidan stood up and pushed his chair back. "I think we're done here."

Jim followed the deputy's lead.

"Mr. Escobar," Aidan said, "I hate to break it to you, but

you did not kill Calvin Lystad. Next time you fire a gun while in a drunken stupor you may not be so fortunate."

Aidan and Jim went back into the hallway.

Jim spoke first. "I don't know who Thomas saw tonight, but it wasn't the mayor."

"The man was swaying. Sounds like just another drunk leaving the bar."

"Or maybe it was Calvin's killer."

11

The two men agreed to start "Jim's first case" in earnest the next morning. At 7:30 am, the snowplows hadn't reached Jim's street yet, so he decided to make the three and a half block slog to work on foot.

The snow had long since stopped falling. The ten inches which lay on the ground looked delicate and shimmery as the morning light hit it. Moisture from the early morning fog had come in contact with the trees and crystallized, encasing each branch and twig in a glorious shimmery layer of ice. There was much beauty to be seen in a North Dakota winter – assuming you were lucky enough to see it before your eyeballs froze in their sockets.

The snowplows were working along Main Street. They had first plowed a path on each side of the street for cars to drive on; creating an eight to twelve foot high snow median down the entire street. From there several bulldozers worked to clean out the medians, dropping load after load into huge open bed trucks. Once full, the trucks would drive to the fairgrounds on the southeastern edge of town. Throughout the winter, the fairgrounds served as the depository for however many thousands of tons of white stuff Mother Nature decided to bless the streets of Kirby with.

Jim entered the *Crier* building just before 8:00. The building was empty. Toni and Layla would arrive around 8:30. Brian would get there when he got there. Jim wrote a note letting the staff know that he would be in and out – mostly out – of the office for the next few days; any problems call the cell. He set the note on the keyboard of Toni's computer. Next Jim grabbed the snow shovel from the closet and went outside to clear the sidewalk in front of the building. As he scooped snow away from the building and toward the curb, he occasionally looked over to the theater next door. Yellow police tape covered the doors. The snow on the sidewalk was shimmery and untouched. "How much of Calvin Lystad's blood is encased in that snow?" he wondered.

Jim was nearly done when Aidan arrived with two coffees from the nearby c-store (that's what North Dakotans call a convenience store).

"Thanks for the coffee," Jim said, huffing a bit from the exertion of shoveling snow.

"These are both for me. I'm using them to keep my hands warm." Aidan smiled and handed him one of the coffees. "Aren't you a little soft for this kind of work?"

"You're welcome to come over and take a shift any time you want."

They went inside. Jim set the shovel by the door, so that someone else could finish clearing the path at some point. They sipped their coffees and talked about the day ahead.

"So what do we do? This is my first murder investigation." Jim took a sip.

"Mine too." Aidan took a sip.

"Do we make a list of suspects? Go over the crime scene? Recreate the events of last night?"

"Did this guy have a wife?"

"Yeah."

"Let's go talk to the wife." Aidan took a sip. "It's usually the wife."

The Lystad home was the nicest one on 4th Avenue South. Not to say it was showy though; folks in North Dakota don't go in for showy. The home looked, in essence, like all of the well-maintained ranch style homes on the block. Only more so.

This morning, both the driveway and the sidewalk running

from the front door to the street had been cleared of snow. Probably a neighbor's way of offering his condolences, Jim figured. He hung back a few steps and let Aidan take the lead. The deputy mounted the two steps up to the porch and rang the doorbell. Almost immediately, the ample and hearty Hazel Lystad appeared in the doorway.

"Thank you so much. I appreciate your – oh." Hazel stopped short; it appeared that she had been expecting someone else. She quickly recovered, "Come on in, boys." She flung open the door and walked back into the house. They followed her in.

"Uff da," Hazel said – rather cheerfully Jim thought – as she hung up the men's coats. "That's quite a pile up we have outside." Hazel led the men into the kitchen, where a veritable banquet of bars, pies, and other treats awaited them.

"Uff da," Jim said, "you've got quite a pile up in here."

"These are just the desserts. The meals are in the fridge. People been dropping them off all morning." In truth, the morning was just beginning – it was barely 9:00. Edible Sympathy – "Empathy" – was expressed early and often in Kirby.

"Jim, your mother brought over tater tot hot dish. And something else I can't remember," Hazel said. Jim cringed inwardly. Tater tot hot dish was not one of Gladys Rosdahl's more successful recipes. Jim hoped that Hazel would never get around to eating it. Hadn't she been through enough already?

Aidan and Jim sat down at the breakfast table while Hazel tore into a pan of some sort of fudgy-caramel, Rice Krispies square concoction. Jim thanked her for the bar and ate it dutifully. Aidan declined a bar.

Hazel poured three cups of coffee – without bothering to ask if anyone wanted some – brought them to the table and sat down. Jim noted that her short gray hair was nicely styled in a tight curl, and she wore a freshly-ironed floral print blouse and dark brown pants. He had entertained the idea that they might find her disheveled, bundled up in a bathrobe, used Kleenex littered throughout the house. The reality was much different. If Hazel Lystad mourned her husband's passing, she was doing an excellent job of hiding that fact.

"I assume you are here on police business," Hazel said. She shifted her eyes to meet Jim's. "Or maybe newspaper business?"

"I can assure you, Mrs. Lystad, that Mr. Rosdahl is here solely as an aid to the Sheriff's Office." Aidan leaned in as if he were letting Hazel in on a secret just between the two of them. "I'm new around here, ma'am, still getting the lay of the land. He's basically just here to help me get to places. Truthfully, I would have left him in the car, if I didn't think he'd freeze out there."

Hazel let out a gentle giggle. Jim ignored the slight. Aidan was apparently playing good cop this morning. Jim wondered if he was supposed to now flip over the table in a screaming rage.

"My condolences on your loss," Aidan said with a sympathetic nod of his head. He switched gears. "What time did your husband leave the house last night, Mrs. Lystad?" Aidan asked.

"Hazel. Around 5:00, Officer..."

"Deputy Aidan Gray. Aidan. You were home when he left?"

"Yes, I'm here all day every day."

"Five o'clock is a little early to leave for a 7:30 meeting."

"He said he had to meet with someone before the city council meeting."

"Who?" Jim asked, reflexively. Hazel looked to him as if she had been at a very lovely picnic and suddenly realized that there were ants on the blanket.

"He didn't tell me, I'm sure. And I didn't ask." Her voice had hardened. She turned her gaze back to Aidan and smiled.

"Do you have any ideas who the meeting might have been with?" Aidan asked.

"I assumed that the council was getting together early to come up with a game plan or something." Hazel paused briefly, making the decision to say the next thing she was going to say. "Or else see that Abby woman he's been carrying on with."

Jim and Aidan both looked down at the floor, neither knowing where else to look. This kind of candor was akin to being a prepubescent boy and having your mother come to your middle school to give your entire health class the sex talk.

Before things could get any more awkward, Jim and Aidan were saved by the bell. The doorbell.

Hazel walked into the living room. From the breakfast table, Jim could still see Hazel as she turned the doorknob. Even before the door was opened all of the way, Hazel had begun speaking. "Thank you so much. I appreciate your coming over." Arms appeared and placed a 9 x 13 Pyrex pan into Hazel's arms. Some words were exchanged from both ends of the doorway. Hazel never invited the whoever-it-was into the house. Moments later, the door closed and Hazel returned to the kitchen with "another damn pan of brownies."

"Where were we?" Hazel asked as she sat back down.

"You believe your husband was having an affair?" Aidan asked.

"Everyone in town saw Cal gallivanting around with that woman. I never did, thank God; but this is a small town. People talk."

Jim – who had felt like the odd man out from the moment he stepped into the Lystad home – ventured another question. "Did you ever confront Calvin about the affair?"

Hazel said "No" without ever taking her eyes off of Aidan. She declined to elaborate.

The relationship between Calvin and Hazel had always perplexed Jim. He had never seen them in public together, though actually Hazel almost never went out at all. Calvin never talked about his wife. They never had children. Some years, Hazel would winter at their home in Arizona while Calvin stayed in Kirby. Other years, they would both go. Jim had often said lightheartedly that there seemed to be no love lost between the Lystads. Now as he listened to Hazel speak, that seemed especially true.

"Do you have any idea who might want to kill your husband?" Aidan asked.

"Beside me?" Hazel smiled. "Abby Quicke."

"Why would you think that?"

"Maybe Cal had ended things with her. She maybe killed him in a jealous range."

Aidan considered this. "That's a lot of maybes."

Hazel's eyes darkened; her affection for Aidan had dissipated with a single comment.

"He never really talked to me about political things," she said coldly, "so if someone stabbed him for being mayor, I wouldn't have any idea. I will say this, whoever it was did it wrong."

"What makes you say that?" Jim asked.

"When you get to the point where you hate someone enough to kill them, I imagine you would want to kill them in the worst possible way."

Aidan asked, "You think the person who did this was desperate to do it?"

Hazel took a sip of coffee. "I meant the worst possible way in the victim's eyes. Some people have a fear of drowning. Some are paranoid about falling from a high place."

"What would have been the best," Jim asked, "I mean, worst way to kill your husband?"

"Poison."

"Calvin had a fear of poisoning?" the deputy asked.

"Not specifically. He was obsessed with – how do I say this? – his insides. Burn his hand on the stove, get a cut on his arm, he was very sensible about how to handle it. But get a cough or feel a pain in his side and he went crazy. He was a hypochondriac when it came to his internal workings. Just like Mabel."

Jim turned to Aidan and said, "Calvin's mother. Deceased."

Hazel continued. "Calvin went all the way to Bismarck at least once a month to get checked out for some new phantom ailment. Uff da, the bills for x-rays, MRIs, genetic testing even." Hazel took another sip of coffee.

After a few more questions, it was apparent to everyone that the conversation was over. The trio made their way back to the living room. They exchanged perfunctory goodbyes as the men put their coats back on. They were nearing the entryway, when the bell rang again.

Hazel opened the door. "Thank you-."

Lois Pedersen burst into the living room and threw her arms around Hazel. "Oh Hazel. He's gone. He's really gone." Lois was weeping and the lines on her face indicated that she had been for some time. Emotional displays such as this were uncommon in these parts. These were tried and true North Dakotans of hearty Norwegian stock – crying was for children and Easterners. Of course, when death showed up at your door, a little license was allowed. Still, this was City Clerk Lois Pedersen. Stoic. Cold. The fifth face on Mount Rushmore. Jim found her emotional display unsettling.

"There, there." Hazel patted Lois on the back. The widow consoling the comforter.

"I woke up this morning, and I thought, and I thought I'd had a terrible dream. But then I realized-" Lois pulled out of the hug and for the first time noticed the two men. She straightened up and wiped at her face.

"I didn't realize you had company."

"Just on our way out," Jim said. "We'll be out of your way."

"Thank you, Mrs. Lystad."

The second that Aidan and Jim were one millimeter passed the threshold, the front door slammed shut. The men descended the steps and walked back to Aidan's squad car.

"Thoughts?" Aidan asked.

"You've got to stop doing that." Jim pointed an accusatory finger at Aidan.

"Doing what?"

"Refusing food." Jim said.

Aidan chuckled. "You're kidding."

"I'm not. In the Romantic Age, you picked a fight by slapping a man with a glove. In North Dakota, you do it by refusing to eat a man's lefse."

"What's lefse?"

Jim sighed. "It's a dessert. A flatbread made from potatoes and flour."

"Sounds gross."

"It's not. It's magical." Jim said. "Do you think Hazel did it?"

"Could have. She doesn't seem too broken up about him being gone."

They got into the car, but Aidan did not start it right away. He was considering something. "Though, she's not exactly a spring chicken."

"So?"

"I'm not sure she'd have the strength to plunge a knife into a man's chest."

Aidan started the car, letting it run a bit before driving.

"I didn't think of that," Jim said. "I guess we can remove Ardis Knutson from the suspect list."

"Who?"

"Nobody. Never mind."

Aidan decided that the car had warmed sufficiently and he drove back toward Main Street. "I have to go back to the office and make a few phone calls," Aidan said. "Want me to drop you off at the paper?"

"That sounds good."

"We can keep going over the case at lunch."

"I'm having lunch with mom today. Would you like to join us?" Jim asked. Aidan smiled. "What's the smile for?"

"Well now, I'm not allowed to refuse, am I? I would love to have lunch with you and your mother. I could use a home cooked meal for a change."

12

Aidan, Jim and Gladys sat in a booth at the Burger Shack waiting for the waitress to come by to take their order. Since the place opened 12 years ago, Jim treating his mom to burgers had become a Thursday tradition – except for about a year during the height of the oil boom. During that time, you had to wait so long for everything: wait for a table to open up, wait for someone to bus away the previous diners' dishes, wait for one overworked waitress to get to your table to take your order, wait for your food, and wait for your check to arrive. Now that things had slowed in the once booming Bakken Formation, other things had sped up. A 72-minute lunch out was back down to 45 minutes.

After the waitress took their food order, the trio in the booth were free to sip their pop and talk about the case.

"What's the first item, boss?" Jim asked. "Write up a list of suspects?"

"We may not have enough napkins."

Jim realized that neither he nor the deputy had brought anything to write on. Or with.

"Not now. We'll get to it." Aidan assured him.

"What have you done so far?" Gladys asked. Her standard abruptness had a brightness to it today. She was enjoying the prospect of being "on the case" with the boys.

"We talked to Hazel this morning." Jim said.

"I don't think she did," Aidan said, "but there's something not right about that woman."

Gladys looked over to a table in the corner, concerned. Jim leaned in toward Aidan and spoke low. "We need to be kind of careful what we say when we're out and about."

"She's not here, is she?" Aidan asked, embarrassed.

"No," Jim whispered, "but see that table over there." Four old hens clucked away, unaware that they were being discussed by folks two tables away.

"Yeah."

"Edith Andrist there is Hazel Lystad's sister." Jim looked at the table again. "I think Edith and Hazel are related to Margaret Stromstad too."

Gladys confirmed this. "Margaret's father and Fern Andrist were cousins."

"Fern was Hazel's mother." Jim explained.

"I'll be more careful," Aidan assured them. "I guess it's true what they say: in a small town everybody knows everybody."

"Not true." Jim smiled. "In a small town everybody's related to everybody."

Aidan got back to business. "Speaking of relatives, did Calvin have any in town? Stick to close relatives for now."

"He and Hazel have no children," Jim said.

"Parents died long ago," Gladys added.

"He has – had – brothers. Two. One moved to Montana, I think. But the oldest brother still runs the Lystad Farm. Peter."

"Paul," Gladys corrected. "Paul's the oldest. Peter's the one in Missoula."

"Are you sure?" Jim asked.

"I guess I would know, then," Gladys said.

"I guess so." Jim turned to Aidan to provide color commentary. "Mom used to watch the Lystad boys when they were kids."

"Foolishness. I was a kid myself," Gladys huffed. "Fourteen years old."

"What was the family like?" Aidan asked, in the same tone as the questions he had addressed to Hazel earlier. Like he was investigating. Jim had serious doubts that his mother's childhood memories would bear light on a murder that had happened less than twenty-four hours ago. You never know, though; some pains cast very long shadows.

"Just a family." Gladys seemed to share her son's skepticism.

"Did they love each other? Did they all get along?"

"They got on, sure." Gladys said, "The boys used to put on little plays for their mother. She was bedridden. And they would go into her room all the time to cheer her up."

"How old were they?"

"Paul was nine. Peter was just a little bit younger. Eight, maybe seven."

"And Calvin?"

"Wasn't born yet. I only worked for them about a year, when Mabel got well enough that she could be up and around. Calvin was born after that."

"And the father?" Aidan asked.

"Ole Lystad," Gladys grunted. "Worthless."

Discussion stopped as the waitress came to the table with their food. As they took their first bites of food, the door opened and two women – one in her mid-twenties and one in her mid-sixties – breezed into the room, gabbing and laughing. Everyone in the place grew quiet and watched with intention as the two women pulled up to two stools at the counter. Soft murmuring rose up from a few tables. A few heads shook in disapproval. The older of the two women had the air of someone much younger. She was lightness and openness, long silver hair and one of those smiles they have in other parts of the world – a smile where you can see the person's teeth.

"That's Abby Quicke," Jim whispered to Aidan who was attempting to extract the ketchup from its bottle, oblivious to the drama unfolding.

Aidan turned to see the counter. "The one on the left?" Jim nodded.

"Doesn't seem too heartbroken to me," Gladys observed. "She probably did it."

"Mom," Jim tried to sound offended even as he let out a slight chuckle. "You sure turned on her in a hurry."

Gladys ignored her son. She looked at the counter long and hard. "Ya. She did it."

"Who's she with?" Aidan asked. Abby's companion was lean and pretty. Jim detected a note in Aidan's voice that made him suspect the question was not purely academic.

"They work together at the abstract, I think," Jim said. "I don't know her name." He looked to his mother. Gladys shook her head. She didn't know the woman either.

"Let's talk to the brother next," Aidan said without taking his eyes from the counter. "But we'll probably want to come back and question her at some point."

"Which of those hers are you referring to?"

Aidan turned to Jim, who was smiling like a Cheshire cat.

13

"Maybe I should take point on this one," Jim said as Aidan's cruiser inched along the icy, narrow dirt path that constituted the road to the Lystad farm.

"Take point?" Aidan was amused. "You watch too much TV."

"I'm just saying Paul isn't much of a talker. At all. Which is nice when you're hunting together. No danger of him scaring off the game. I think he might be more inclined to give us information if he's talking to someone he already knows."

"All right, you can have this one. But if he makes a break for it and we have to tail the perp, I take point. Roger that?" Aidan smiled.

"Roger."

The Lystad farm didn't get much traffic, so Paul Lystad had noticed the deputy's vehicle creeping up the road while it was still a ways off. When the car finally stopped in front of the house, Paul was standing outside waiting to receive them. With his lanky body dressed in a flannel shirt and overalls, he looked not unlike a scarecrow. With his tight-set jaw on a face made ancient by years of working out in the elements, those crows wouldn't have been scared; they would've been downright terrified.

"Quite a storm last night," Jim said as he got out of the car. Paul nodded. "This is Deputy Aidan Gray."

"Good afternoon, Mr. Lystad." Aidan said.

"Afternoon," Paul said.

"We wanted to come by and first say how sorry we are for your loss" Jim took point. Paul nodded again, as Jim continued. "Calvin was a good man."

This comment elicited a half snort from Paul Lystad.

Aidan was shaking from the cold. He inched ever so slightly toward the house, but the other two men stood firm. Paul, a man in his seventies, was wearing jeans and only a long-sleeved shirt.

Jim changed topics, moving from the personal to the general. "Snow came earlier than expected."

"Ya."

"I don't suppose that's doing you any good schedule-wise."

"Don't suppose."

Aidan couldn't take it anymore. "Is there any chance we could take this conversation inside?"

"Ya." Paul Lystad turned around and walked toward the house.

Jim leaned in toward Aidan. "We're lucky that we caught him in a talkative mood," he said without a hint of sarcasm.

The men went into the living room and sat down. To Aidan, the house was only negligibly warmer than the outside. The house was ancient – having no central heat or air. A wood stove in the center provided heat for the entire house. The Lystads had elected not to have that stove burning at this particular time. When Paul's wife, Elizabeth, offered the men some coffee, Aidan practically screamed his "yes."

"I didn't see you at the city council meeting last night," Jim observed.

"Ya, ya, no." After a long pause. "That stuff don't matter to me, now."

"Were you here at home all night?"

"Ya."

Elizabeth entered with the coffee. "We were both here." She distributed the mugs and went back into the kitchen so the men could be alone.

"Never left the house?" Jim asked.

"Ya, no."

"Who do you think might have killed your brother?" Jim

cut to the chase.

"No idea, now."

"You don't know of anybody who might have wanted to see Calvin dead?" Aidan asked.

"Ya, no."

Aidan himself could think of a half dozen murder suspects and he'd only been in town a month. Paul was either in serious denial or he was lying.

"So Calvin got along with most folks?" Aidan asked.

Paul did his half snort again. "No."

"But you just said-"

Here Paul cut Aidan off. "That ain't the same as murdering someone, now."

"It's a good start," Aidan assured him.

Paul shook his head. "Cal wouldn't've never been born, then."

Jim asked, "What do you mean by that, Paul?"

Paul simply shrugged and took a sip of his coffee.

Aidan and Jim's side of the conversation continued for a few more minutes, but Paul had fallen mute. He had already expended quite a few words today; like all good hunters he knew that when you hit your limit, you stopped.

The men stood and made their way to the door. "Oh, I just want to pop into the kitchen and thank Elizabeth for the coffee," Jim said. Paul walked a reluctant Aidan back out into the cold, while Jim rounded the corner into the kitchen.

Unlike the rest of the house, the kitchen had all the modern conveniences, having been newly remodeled sometime during the Carter administration.

Elizabeth's back was to Jim. She was busy at work; she had the oven going and two of the four stove burners heating up pots.

"The coffee was wonderful. Thank you so much."

Elizabeth turned around in surprise. "Of course, Jim. You boys done, then?"

"Yes, ma'am."

"Be careful out in this weather." Elizabeth wrung her hands in a dishtowel. Whether it was from nervousness or simply to dry them, Jim could not tell. "I can't believe Calvin's gone. Such a shame."

"Can I just ask one more thing before we get out of your hair?"

"Surely."

"You were both here the entire night?"

"Yes."

"Neither of you ever left the house at any point."

"No, no-. Well, ya," Elizabeth reconsidered. "Around 6:00, Paul got a call from a neighbor that one of our cows had gotten loose and was out on the highway. Paul went out to get it."

"What time did he get back?"

"7:00? 7:30" She said without certainty.

"Which neighbor called?"

"Pedersen, I think."

"Arley?" Jim asked even though he knew it couldn't be anyone else. Elizabeth nodded. Arley and Lois Pedersen had their own farm nearby.

"Thank you. Again, sorry for your lose. Have a good day." Jim turned to go. He made it to the door before stopping once more. "Do you know what Paul was talking about when he said Calvin was hated even before he was born?"

"Uff da!" Elizabeth exclaimed. "That husband of mine. Always running his mouth off. Never knows when to quit." The two people standing in that kitchen had two very different perceptions of Paul Lystad.

"Paul's mother had rheumatic fever when he was young. The poor soul was bedridden for over a year. Just as she was getting better, she got pregnant with Calvin. After he was born, she went back to taking care of the home, but she was never the same woman. Only lived another seven years or so. Poor dear was only in her forties. I can't imagine."

"She blamed Calvin for never recovering fully?"

"Something like that. I didn't know the woman. I didn't meet Paul until college in Grand Forks." Elizabeth lowered her head. She treated the admission of not being born in Kirby like something you would only admit to your priest. "But I can tell you none of the other Lystads got on with Calvin. Not Paul, not Peter, not even their father, Ole. I assume it was the same way with Mabel. Calvin was the black sheep."

"That's odd," Jim said.

"I suppose every family has one."

"True. But the youngest child? If anything Claudette always favored our youngest."

Even though she was standing a good eight feet from Jim, Elizabeth leaned in conspiratorially, "I did too."

Jim thanked Elizabeth again for the coffee. He made his way outside where Paul and a shivering Aidan were engaged in a staring contest. After the men exchanged goodbyes for grunts, Jim and Aidan got back inside the cruiser.

"That was an awful long 'thank you'." Aidan said as he inched along the road back to the highway.

"You interviewed the wrong Lystad."

14

The men returned to Kirby. Aiden dropped Jim off at *The Crier*. Jim needed to pop in to get some work done and to make sure the whole place hadn't burned down to the ground. He rarely spent this much time away from the office, except when he slept or was out of town. Even on weekends, Jim spent most of the day alone in the *Crier* building.

Aidan and Jim made plans to meet up in the evening to go over the details of the case so far and come up with a game plan for where to go from there. "And make a list of suspects?" Jim asked.

"Yes," Aidan agreed, "it's time to make your precious list of suspects."

Jim realized how much he was enjoying this. *I would have made a great detective*, he thought but immediately knew he was lying to himself. *I would have made a great TV detective*, he amended the thought.

He came in to find the office overrun with envelopes and invoices. *The Crier* did their billing one day a month and this was that day. Toni sat at her desk, folding invoices and stuffing them into envelopes. Layla sat at the bookkeeper's desk. She was sealing the already stuffed envelopes and placing stamps on each. This was the bookkeeper's job, a position that was vacant at present. Toni and Layla, mostly Toni, were filling in the gap temporarily until a new bookkeeper could be found. The current definition of "temporarily" was four months and counting.

"Been able to hold down the fort without me?" Jim asked.

"Oh, have you not been here? Didn't notice." Toni replied.

"Only about a hundred people have come in wondering

where you are." Layla informed him.

"Messages on your desk," said Toni.

"Did Brian and his mother-in-law ever make it back from Minot?" Jim asked.

Toni shrugged. "He hasn't been in."

Jim went into his "office" – a tiny 3' x 6' room just past the other desks. There was room for a desk and a small file cabinet and not much else. Jim picked up a small stack of messages. He thought better of going through them and set the stack back on the desk. He picked up the office phone and made a call.

"Hey Jim," came Brian from the other end.

"Hey Brian. You doing okay?"

"That storm was a little scary last night. We were on our way to Minot to pick up Judith's mother when it started coming down. We ended up staying overnight; didn't want to take a chance on the roads."

"Probably a wise decision," Jim agreed. "You guys heading back today?"

"Yeah, got in about 11:00 this morning. The highway was looking fine by then."

"You didn't come in today." Jim rubbed his temple with his free hand.

"Figured the day was kind of a wash at that point."

"Come in."

"Sure, Jim. What's up?"

"Your job!" is what Jim wanted to yell into the phone. Instead, he said, "I'm going to be out of the office quite a bit over the next few days."

"Helping out on the murder investigation?"

How on earth could Brian have heard about that already? Jim asked himself. *It's a small town,* Jim answered himself.

"Glad I wasn't there," Brian continued. "Hard to believe someone would kill old Calvin."

"I'm going to need everyone else helping to pick up the

slack while I'm out."

"You betcha, Jim. I'll be in soon."

Jim hung up the phone. He propped his arms up, resting his elbows on the desk and buried his head in his hands.

"Should I come back another time?"

Jim turned to see Dennis Anderson standing in the doorway. The hospital administrator wore a light blue button up shirt with tie and a pair of black jeans. Rural Formal.

On a good day, Jim disliked Dennis Anderson. But after his phone conversation, Jim was feeling downright angry at the prospect of dealing with another creep. In true Norwegian style, Jim suppressed his rage. "This is a fine time, Dennis. Have a seat."

Dennis looked in the direction of Toni and Layla who were mere feet away. "Could we talk in the back?"

"Sure."

The two went to the table in back and sat down. "I hear you've been deputized and are working on Calvin Lystad's murder case," Dennis said. He had a voice that possessed only one volume level: Loud. Jim wondered what the point of moving to the conference was; he was sure the ladies could hear Dennis even from back here.

"I'm no deputy. I'm just helping the new guy get around town."

"Oh," Dennis wasn't sure how to proceed.

"Did you know Calvin very well? On a personal level, I mean."

"Not as such, no."

"Me neither. He'd come in here a lot, though. Mostly on Wednesdays after he'd seen the paper. He'd come to my desk and let me know all the ways I'd gotten the story wrong and how I had taken his quotes out of context."

"That must have been frustrating," Dennis said.

"Half the town comes in here to complain on any given month." Jim smiled. "You get used to it. Calvin would leave saying that from now on he'd only give direct answers to direct questions. Two days later, he'd forgot all about it. We'd be in the back here, him going on about all the nonsense he had to deal with as mayor."

"I suppose I was a part of that 'nonsense'." Dennis mused.

"You're name might have come up." Jim conceded.

"Jim, the reason I came by is I suppose I'm on your list of suspects."

Jim thought, *You will be if we ever make one.*

Dennis continued. "I figured it's only a matter of time before you come talking to me. Thought I would beat you to it."

"Why are you bringing this to me, Dennis?" Something deeper than the investigation hung in the air between them that they both elected to ignore. . . for now. "Take this directly to someone in the Sheriff's Office."

"It must look suspicious that I wasn't at the city council meeting last night."

"I don't know if I'd say suspicious," Jim said. "But I did notice it."

"I had every intention of going. In fact, I was working late at the hospital preparing my remarks for the meeting. When it was time to head over, the storm had picked up. I didn't want to risk it, so I hunkered down there."

Jim found this hard to believe. Sure, if Dennis were a Texan seeing that snow come in sideways and four inches already on the ground, he'd hightail it back inside. If Dennis were from Kansas, the snow would have given him pause. But Dennis was born and bred in Kirby, North Dakota; if he had somewhere important to be, a couple of billion flakes weren't going to slow him down. There were over a hundred Kirbyites in the L&C Theater the night before to prove that.

"Other people saw you at the hospital, I suppose."

"Mr. Park did. Around 7:50, he popped his head into my office. I was playing solitaire on my computer. He let me know the time, and asked what I was still doing there. I told him that

I didn't want to risk it. I was hunkering down for the night. I slept in my office. I didn't see anyone else until the morning."

Jim noted the repeated "didn't want to risk it" and "hunkered down." This story was rehearsed. That didn't necessarily mean it was a lie – Dennis Anderson liked to be prepared – but it certainly could have been. "No one came and got you when Calvin was brought in?"

Dennis had not prepared for Jim's question. "I, uh, no. I'm not a doctor. I couldn't have treated the man."

"No, but it's a pretty high-profile patient. They'd want to bring you into the loop."

"I don't suppose anyone else knew I was even there."

"Except Mr. Park."

"Yes, except Mr. Park," Dennis agreed. "I think he was on his way out himself, when he saw me. Probably wasn't there when Calvin came in."

"Ya. Could be."

Dennis stood. "Anyway, I just wanted to stop by and lay it all out there. The last thing I would want you to think is that I have anything to hide."

15

"Dennis Anderson is hiding something," Jim asserted.

It was just after 8:00 pm. A mere 24 hours after Calvin Ly-stad collapsed onto the floor of the L&C Movie Theater. Jim and Aidan were together in Jim's living room. The décor was in a style known as French Country. Framed pictures – of Jim and Claudette, the boys, Marlin and Gladys Rosdahl, Clau-dette's parents – adorned the walls and every available sur-face.

Jim sat at the secretary in the corner which served as the home office. He had pen in hand, and a pad of paper before him. With interest, Aidan perused the selection of books on the two large bookcases.

"Are you even listening to me?"

"Yeah." Aidan's eyes never left the books. "Hiding some-thing."

"Anybody else I should add to the list?"

Aidan turned to Jim. "What about that guy at the hospital? Anderson."

"That's who I was just talking about?"

"Oh."

"What has you so endlessly fascinated over there?"

Aidan turned back to the books and smiled. "I gotta say. It's all starting to make sense now."

"What is?"

Aidan ran his fingers along the line of books. "Agatha Chris-tie. Tony Hillerman. Dorothy Sayers. You were just dying for a murder to come along, weren't you?"

"Dying? That's cute. Those are Claudette's books."

"You've never read them?"

"If I've got nothing else to read."

Aidan laughed. He pulled a book from the shelf. "Look at this. *Pick Your Poison: A History of Hemlock, Herbs, and Other Silent Killers.*" He shook his head, smiling. "You're morbid."

"It's very informative. And actually an entertaining read."

"I'm sure." Aidan opened the book to a random spot and began to read. "'The Emperor Domitian allegedly poisoned his niece, Julia, in an effort to abort their incestuous love child.' Good read. Fun for the whole family." Aidan closed the book and returned it to the shelf.

Jim chuckled and made his way over to the bookcase. "No, there's a lot of fascinating stories in here. There was this guy in India who used to convince strangers to eat poisonous datura seeds. They would die and then he would rob them."

"How does one convince strangers to eat poison?" Aidan's voice exuded skepticism.

"He would eat a small amount first to show them that it was safe. He had built up a resistance over the years. But he ended up taking too much and dying himself."

"Crime's a rough racket."

Jim was thumbing through the book now, trying to find a certain passage. "And during the Eisenhower administration – I think it was – they thought the U.S. Ambassador to Italy was being poisoned because she was complaining about irrational behavior and feeling drunk. Or something. Anyway, it turned out that there was arsenic in the ceiling material of her home. It was being shook loose by the laundromat on the floor above." Jim was exuberant.

"They made an ambassador live below a laundromat?"

Jim looked at Aidan sourly. "That's what you get out of that story?"

Aidan took the book out of Jim's hands, closed it, and placed it back onto the shelf. "You're getting off on this?"

"Don't be ridiculous." Despite his words, Jim couldn't deny

the hint of joy in his voice. He felt a twinge of guilt. Jim returned to his seat in the corner.

"When a murder finally came to your door, you must have been dying to get involved." Now Aidan was the one getting pleasure. "You think this whole thing is going to end with some climactic scene where all of the suspects are gathered in one room, and you lay out the details of your investigation piece by piece."

"Very funny." Jim wasn't amused.

"Until you finally get to the end. You point to the butler and say," Aidan fell into a bad English accent, "'The butler did it. Take him away inspector'."

"We don't have a lot of butlers in Kirby." Jim said.

"You know, it's not like they make it out in the books. You can't just look a man up and down like Sherlock Holmes and deduce 'You were born on a Thursday'."

"I know that." Jim tried to smile.

"Sure. But deep down you're thinking 'I'm a clever guy. I'm clever enough to do this'. So go ahead." Aidan threw his hands into the air, on display for Jim. "Sherlock Holmes me."

"What?"

"Use your keen powers of deduction on me. Tell me three things that the average person wouldn't know just by looking at me."

"You're insane."

"That's one. Two more."

Reluctantly, Jim stood and looked Aidan over. He was a clever guy. And deep down he did think he was clever enough to be an investigator. If he worked hard enough.

He studied Aidan carefully. There were dirt smudges on his collar. Aha! That meant he was wearing the same shirt he'd worn yesterday. Or maybe it was just a stubborn stain that didn't come out in the wash. A small scar graced Aidan's head just behind his left ear. Had he been in a fight some time back? Or could it be a surgical scar?

"I'm waiting," Aidan said with a smile.

"Perfection takes time." Jim circled Aidan a few times, then stopped to face him. "Okay, I'm ready."

"Three things. Shoot."

"One. The scar on your neck indicates that when you were young you used to get into a lot of fights. Two. The creased pants and the smudge on your collar tell me that you keep a home that is very organized even if isn't very clean. Three. You, in fact, were born on a Thursday."

Aidan smiled as he lowered his arms.

"How'd I do?" Jim asked.

"One out of three. Not too bad. How did you know I was born on a Thursday?"

"I figured when you made that joke, the first day that would pop into your head would be the day you were born. If you knew it."

"Not bad."

"You think you could do better? Say something about me that the average person doesn't know."

"I'm starting to doubt there's anything people don't know about anybody in this town." Aidan said. He strained to sound lighthearted.

"Come on?"

"Nah. I don't claim to be Sherlock."

"You're the real investigator. Investigate."

"Let's get back to the suspect list."

"I'll make it easy on you. One thing."

Aidan looked in Jim's eyes. Jim was a dog with a bone. He was not going to let go of this until Aidan played along. Aidan looked at the ground as he spoke. "Your wife in Bismarck-"

"Everyone knows that. I've told you that."

"-she has no plans to return here."

Jim paled. He placed his hand on the secretary to steady himself and lowered himself back into his chair.

"I'm sorry. It was a stupid thing for me to blurt out." Aidan took a seat on the couch. The two men sat in silence.

After a minute, Jim spoke. "Claudette never liked it here. Too small. Too isolated. Everyone in your business all the time. We moved here when my dad died. We had too. Mom, who's tough as nails just fell apart. And there was no one left to run the paper. I couldn't let it die too." As he spoke, Jim looked at the wall in front of him. Although Aidan was the only one in the room, Jim did not seem to be addressing him particularly. "Claudette looked at it like I chose *The Crier* over her. I think the boys were the only thing keeping her here, really. Once they were both gone, she had no more reason to be with me."

"I'm sorry, Jim."

"Don't. It's almost a relief. It's the first time I've spoken it aloud."

"You haven't told anyone?"

"Mom knows, but we've never discussed it. She knows, though."

"I didn't think it was possible to keep secrets here."

"It's not. Only a matter of time before Candy Gillund at the post office puts it together, if she hasn't already. I just want to hold onto it for as long as I can. Let my pain be my own, and not some anecdote."

Eventually the two men got back to work. Aidan went over the official findings so far. It wasn't much. Calvin Lystad had suffered a single stab wound to the chest. The murder weapon had an eight to ten inch blade, likely a kitchen knife. The knife had not been recovered. It was nearly impossible to determine the location from which Calvin had come to the theater. His tracks and any blood spilled were covered by the snow and/or moved by the heavy winds.

Next came the suspect list. Calvin's brother Paul and his widow Hazel were on the top of the list. "You said it's usually a relative. Should I work up a list of Calvin's extended family?" Jim had asked. Aidan shook his head. "That's going to end up being the entire county. Let's just focus on immediate family and people with motive."

The list grew. Dennis Anderson, hospital administrator. Abby Quicke, the happiest jilted lover of all time. Tomás Escobar, the oil man. He seemed unlikely at this point, but couldn't be ruled out entirely.

"And there's that crazy guy." Aidan suddenly remembered.

"You'll have to be more specific."

"The land guy. The eminent domain thing."

"Bud Legaard?"

"If that's his name."

"Bud Legaard is in his eighties. He wouldn't have been able to stab Calvin in the chest."

"He might have been able to."

"Sure, if Calvin had just stood there and let him."

Aidan smiled. "You don't think the mayor would have done that?"

"Maybe last year. But not yesterday."

"Why last year?"

"It was an election year. Calvin would do just about anything to get someone's vote." Jim remembered something. "Doesn't matter if he has the strength or not. Bud's already in Arizona for the winter."

Aidan looked at the list they had composed so far. "Who else?"

"Could someone who was at the meeting have done it?"

Aidan considered this. "I don't see how. Not unaided. The mayor likely collapsed several minutes after being stabbed. You thinking of that city clerk?"

"Lois? She seemed pretty distraught this morning at Hazel's."

"It was a little over the top. Maybe regret over what she'd done. Or maybe she's just a good actress."

Jim laughed. "Lois Pedersen is full Norwegian on both sides of her family."

"So?"

"So, it's hard enough for us to produce tears when we're actually sad. Doing it just for the fun of it is out of the question."

"Her husband maybe. The farmer." Aidan said.

"Arley? Why? What's his motive?"

"Maybe he was in cahoots with the brother, Paul. You said Arley called him last night about a stray cow. What if it was a signal that it was time to take care of Calvin?"

"Seems like stretching."

"Stretching is good exercise." Aidan smiled. "Who were you thinking of, from the meeting?"

"I don't know."

Aidan gave Jim a skeptical look. "Bull."

"Ryan Peterson, I guess," Jim admitted. "The councilman. I feel weird saying it; we're friends. But there was no love lost between those two. Ryan hated Calvin personally and professionally. And now that Calvin's dead, Ryan will likely step in as mayor. Which he's always wanted."

"This Ryan any relation to Arley and Lois?"

"No, why?"

"I just wondered since they have the same last name."

Jim laughed at this. After describing to Aidan the differences in the spelling and the imperceptibly minute variance in pronunciation of the two names, Jim added Ryan Peterson and Arley Pedersen to the list of suspects.

The next day would be Friday. The guys decided that they would speak to Abby Quicke in the morning, and then to Ryan Peterson after that. That's as far as the game plan went.

The men each had a bottle of beer and were catching the high school sports highlights on the 10:00 o'clock news. Jim opened the small side table drawer, pulling out two cigars and a lighter.

"Care for one?" he asked Aidan.

"Don't mind if I do." Aidan took one of the cigars.

"Claudette never let me smoke these in the house." Jim bit the end of the cigar and spit it onto the carpet in defiance. Aidan laughed as Jim put fire to his stogie.

"Do we continue investigating on the weekend?" Jim asked as he lit Aidan's cigar.

Aidan took a few puffs to get the thing going. "I was planning on it."

"Good. That gives us three solid days to solve this case."

"Don't get me wrong, the sooner we wrap this up the better, but we can't really dictate when this thing gets sorted out."

"We need to. I have to put the paper together on Monday and Tuesday."

Aidan laughed.

"I'm serious. I won't be able to do anything else either of those days."

Aidan got suddenly serious. "That might help us actually."

Jim straightened. "How so?"

Aidan leaned in. "We think this guy is a local, right?"

"Right?"

"He probably knows that the paper is put together on Mondays and Tuesdays."

"Most people do."

"So, if we don't have it figured out by Sunday afternoon, he'll probably step forward and confess so that it doesn't mess up your schedule."

Jim looked at Aidan as he burst into his hearty non-Norwegian laugh.

16

By Friday, the temperature in Kirby had jumped up into the high 40s. The ice on the streets was melting away. The snow on the ground was starting to give way to mud. (In most of the world, when snow melts it becomes water; in North Dakota, snow turns directly into mud.) Natives threw off their coats entirely. Non-natives took off their heavy winter parkas and donned their light winter parkas.

At 9:00 that morning, Jim Rosdahl and a lightly-parka-ed Aidan Gray walked over to the Clark County Abstract on Main Street across from Jen's Yarn Barn. The Abstract's function was to research the titles on land – determining who property belonged to, previous owners, who owned the mineral rights, and so forth. That one on the list just before "so forth" was what had kept the ladies of the Clark County Abstract hoping for the past few years. Everybody and their mother had wanted to make a buck on this oil boom. The select few who actually did were either those who worked for an oil company that leased out the mineral rights from certain lucky North Dakotans or those lucky North Dakotans who found they had mineral rights to lease. Recently the work load had settled down near its pre-boom levels; but the next boom was always around the corner. These things ran in cycles.

Jim and Aidan entered the building. The large front room had at one time been the lobby of a bank. It now housed the desks of the four women who researched and wrote up the abstracts. Their boss, Kara Unhjem, kept herself in the old bank manager's office. Abby was standing at the second desk, arranging items, getting her desk and her mind prepped for another day.

The desk closest to the door was occupied by the pretty

young woman who had accompanied Abby at lunch the previous day. Aidan lit up when he saw her. "Good morning, miss."

She smiled. "Good morning, officer." She made a cursory glance in Jim's direction, "Morning."

"How are you doing this morning?" Aidan led.

"Autumn. Smith. And I'm doing well, thank you. What can I help you with this morn-"

"Aidan. Deputy Aidan Gray."

Jim was done with this. He called over to the second desk. "Abby, you got time to talk to us?"

When Aidan told her that it would be better if they talked in private, Abby suggested they walk outside. Most businesses in Kirby were not built for privacy; why bother, everybody knew everybody's business soon enough anyway. Aidan, Jim and Abby headed south on Main Street; there would be less foot traffic than if they went north toward the drug store and the post office.

"She's single," were Abby's first word once they were outside. She addressed Aidan.

"Who?"

"Autumn. Smith." She smiled as she imitated her coworker, but there was nervousness behind it.

"I'll keep that in mind." Aidan gave a slight smile, then grew serious. "Mrs. Quicke, we need to ask you a few questions?"

"Is this about Mayor Lystad?" Abby's nervousness grew.

"Yes."

"You found out about our dealings?" Abby asked. Jim was reminded once again that Abby was not from Kirby originally. She was answering the questions before they were asked, volunteering personal information. Behavior unbecoming a Norwegian.

"I wouldn't have used the word 'dealings,' but yes?"

Abby was all nerves now. Her breath was heavy, her smile

gone, and all life had left her face. "Are you going to arrest me?"

Aidan stopped walking momentarily. The directness of the question had thrown him. Abby and Jim stopped and turned to Aidan. "It depends. Can you tell me where you were on Wednesday night between 7:00 and 8:30?"

"I'm at the school every night until about 9:00. And then I go home."

"You teach night classes or something?"

Jim stepped in. "Abby and her husband are restoring an old one-room schoolhouse south of Mackenzie."

"We're hoping to live in it if we can ever get the thing finished. And get the town to sign off on rezoning."

"So your husband was with you on Wednesday night?" Aidan asked. "He can verify your whereabouts?"

"Most nights it's just me. Hank is a very capable craftsman but let's just say, he isn't a workaholic." Abby's smiled returned momentarily, and then a flash of understanding squelched it again. "Wait a minute. Wednesday night. You think I killed the mayor?"

Jim saw Ardis Knutson and Ardis Knudsvig on the other side of the street, heading north. Their already snail-like pace slowed when they saw Jim, Aidan and Abby huddled together. "Let's keep walking," Jim suggested. It's harder for folks to hit a moving target.

The walk continued. "I didn't kill Mayor Lystad. Why would I kill...the man hadn't even paid me yet."

"Paid you? Are you confessing to prostitution?" Aidan couldn't keep the shock out of his voice.

"That's vulgar," Abby snorted. "I admit, I compromised my-"

Jim cut her off. "Hang on. Hang on. I think we're having two separate conversations here. Let's try this again. Abby, were you and Calvin having an affair?"

Abby froze in her tracks. Jim and Aidan stopped walking

and turned to face Abby. That face was featureless, dead. She looked from Jim to Aidan and back again. "You think I was carrying on an affair with Calvin Lystad?"

Neither of the men responded.

"Who told you that?" Abby asked.

"No one in particular," Jim said.

Abby nodded in understanding. "That's just the general consensus around town."

Again, the men did not respond. Abby's eyes moved between the men. And then it happened. Abby Quicke exploded with laughter. Loud, uncontrollable laughter. It was one of those laughs that causes your body to double over. Jim was afraid for a moment that Abby might end up splayed on the sidewalk at the end of it. Eventually, the laughter slowed and Abby seemed to regain control of her movements. As the laughter devolved into a sporadic chuckling, she wiped the tears away from her eyes.

Jim looked across the street. Ardis and the other Ardis had ceased their walking. They were joined by a few other lookiloos. Jim wanted to keep moving.

"I'll take that as a denial of the affair," Aidan said.

"Officer, I am devoted to Hank Quicke. He may be a slug, but he's my slug, and I love him. And until the day either George Clooney or Idris Elba move to North Dakota, that isn't going to change. An affair with Calvin Lystad? Ha." Abby didn't laugh that time; she actually spoke the word "ha."

The group started walking again. "If you weren't having an affair-" Aidan started.

"If I was going to start something on the side, I'd at least hold out for someone who bathes more than twice a week."

Jim smiled. He had always found Abby amusing, though he believed her joke was probably not grounded in fact. Sure, Calvin always dressed as if he had just come in from the fields, but based on what Hazel had said about his obsession with health Jim thought it unlikely that Calvin exercised poor hygiene.

"Abby," Aidan's voice broke Jim's rabbit-trailing thought, "why did you think I came here to arrest you?"

"Um, well," Abby stumbled. "For the mayor's murder. Like you said."

"No," Jim said, "we threw you off with this murder talk. You thought we'd come for you for something else." He turned the group left onto 2nd Avenue South, into a residential area, and away from the prying eyes of Main Street.

"No, that's...I was just confused."

"Some 'dealings' that you had with Calvin," Aidan said.

"That he never paid you for," Jim added. Abby couldn't hide from her own words. *This is why Norwegians don't talk about themselves*, Jim thought, *it's easier to get away with murder.*

"I don't want to go to jail." Abby turned a pleading face to the newspaper man, "I'm too old to go to jail, Jim."

"Abby, what did you do?"

They continued to walk in silence – one of those silences where you feel the air change. Abby finally managed to break that silence, however softly.

"Calvin Lystad hired me to do research on some land."

"That is what the Abstract does," Jim said.

"But he didn't hire the Abstract. He hired me. Off hours and off the record."

"Why?"

"He came to me several months ago. He wanted to know the history of a number of properties – ownership, transfers, mineral rights. The whole work up."

"Was this his land you were researching?"

"His family farm. But all the quarters surrounding it too: the Lund farm, Bud Legaard's, the Pedersens' and another one."

"Bakke," Jim filled in the blank. His family's farm on his mother's side.

"Yes, Bakke. There were a couple of other properties north of town, too."

"I guess I don't know enough about all this land stuff," Aidan said. "What was Lystad's play?"

"He didn't tell me. But he seemed to believe, or at least he made me believe that it was going to end up in a big payday for him. Once he made out, I'd get paid a handsome fee."

"Mineral rights?" Jim asked.

"I assume so," Abby said. "I was fine not knowing. The less I had to be invested in that man's life, the better."

"I don't understand what claims he would have on those other farms." Aidan felt out of his element.

"Those five farms are divided strangely. None of them is a true quarter. I thought it might be-"

"Excuse me," Aidan interrupted, "What do you mean when you say 'quarter'?"

"Sorry. During the Homestead days, the government divided the land into quarter sections – 160 acres – and sold the quarters for $200 each."

"Two hundred dollars for 160 acres? So the government had to basically beg people to live here?" Aidan mused. "That sounds about right."

"There was a lot of buying and selling of sections of the land between these five farms during the 20s and 30s. My guess is they were doing it to help each other stay out of foreclosure. As a result, none of the properties have a full 160 acres and each of them lies in at least two sections as they were originally laid out in the homestead days."

Aidan rubbed his temple. "Let's cut to the chase. Are you saying that the Lund farm may be owned by someone else?"

"They own the land. But they may not own the minerals underneath."

"How is that possible?" Aidan asked.

"When a landowner dies, he might will the land to one child and the mineral rights to another. He might sell off the mineral rights in order to keep the land. Many of these farms were in foreclosure back in the Great Depression. If homeowners turned to the Federal Land Bank for assistance, they lost half their minerals right then and there."

"Abby, who owns the minerals on these farms?" Jim asked.

"I don't know. I was still digging when the mayor died."

"What about the other properties you mentioned?"

"Hadn't even started on those."

"Ah, this is giving me a headache," Aidan said.

They decided at this point to turn around and head back. The return trip was made in relative silence until they stopped in front of the Abstract Building. "Am I going to jail?" Abby looked deep into Jim's eyes.

"I'm not the one to ask."

Abby turned her gaze to Aidan. "To be honest," Aidan said, "I don't really understand most of this. You may have done something illegal here, but I'm not entirely sure what it is. And quite frankly, ma'am, I have bigger fish to fry right now."

Abby smiled with relief. "If there is anything I can do to help you guys out, please let me know."

Jim had an idea of how she could. They went into her boss's office and asked Kara Unhjem for permission to have Abby Quicke do some research for them. It might be important to their case. Kara was happy to oblige them, all of the resources of the Clark County Abstract were at their disposal.

They thanked Kara, leaving out the part about half the work already being done.

17

Jim and Aidan left the Abstract and headed north on Main Street.

"I don't really understand what any of that was," Aidan admitted. "I'm just going to go back to thinking she was sleeping with the guy."

The comment was a joke, but Jim treated it seriously. "I wouldn't think a woman would refer to her lover as 'Mayor Lystad'."

They passed the post office and stopped at the Penney Building. Aidan grabbed the latch. Jim pressed his weight on the door to keep Aidan from opening it. "Maybe I should sit this one out," Jim said. "Ryan and I are friends."

Aidan let go of the latch. "Are you afraid he won't answer your questions?"

"I'm more afraid that I won't ask my questions."

"Relax, Jim. I don't think this guy did it. He may have had the motive, but he's a million miles from having the means."

Jim hesitated.

Aidan shrugged. "It's up to you."

"Oh, I can make other friends. Let's go fry this bastard," Jim muttered followed by a sigh.

"That's the spirit."

The J.C. Penney Company opened a retail store in Kirby, North Dakota in 1926. In those days the company's strategy included providing service to small and medium-sized cities. Seeing as those are the only kind of cities you'll find in North Dakota, the state abounded with J.C. Penneys. Eventually, company executives decided – like so many company executives before them – that J.C. Penney was wasting its time dealing with these small potatoes. Large cities were where it was at. So in the early 1980s, the company started leaving the small towns. Kirby was one of the first casualties.

The Penney building in Kirby lay dormant nearly two years after that, until Eunice Nielsen decided to fill the void and open a shop that sold ladies' apparel. Unfortunately, Eunice failed to realize that the void had already been filled – Jen's Yarn Barn having shifted their focus from crafts to clothing. Eunice's store closed after about a year. Then it became a bakery. When that closed, Hannah Imhoff opened a thrift store. "Hannah-Me-Downs" folded for a lack of donations; people in North Dakota never throw things out. Around this time the second floor of the building was converted into seven apartments, which filled quickly. Most people in Kirby own, but those who rent apparently wanted to be a part of the "downtown scene." In the 1990s, the first floor became an arcade. The second-floor residents soon complained about the noise, and the arcade was forced to shut down. It lay vacant for a few more years. Then it reopened as a five-and-dime, though the days of things costing a nickel or a dime were long gone. It had several more iterations after that: a travel agency, a diner, another clothing shop, then a place that sold lighthearted Scandinavian-themed souvenirs such as "Uff da" magnets and books with titles like *A Norwegian's Guide to Surviving Lutefisk*. Currently the structure housed an insurance agency.

Despite the building's rich history, today, if you ask a local what sits at the southwest corner of Main and 1st Avenue North, he or she will tell you, "the Penney Building." North Dakotans have a hard time letting go.

"Making the rounds. I was wondering when you guys would get to me," part-time Councilman and full-time insurance agent, Ryan Peterson said as he welcomed them into his office. Ryan looked like a politician – and an insurance agent – a little too handsome, a little too polished, a little too friendly. He had an air of youthfulness. In his mid-forties, you'd probably mistake him for a man ten years younger. It was only when he grinned too wide, that the age lines showed around his eyes and mouth.

Ryan led them to a small round table and the men sat. "It's such a shame about Cal. He was a good man. What his loss means to his family and this community..." Ryan shook his head. Jim supposed that these were the kindest words about Calvin Lystad that Ryan had ever strung together in his whole life.

"Yes, well." Aidan pulled out a black notepad and a pen. "I've read the statement you gave to Sheriff Bakke on the night of the murder. I just want to fill that in a little bit."

"Okay."

"When did you arrive at the meeting?"

"About 6:45. Andrea Dhuyvetter and I arrived early to set up the tables. Jon got there about seven, which is when we expected the mayor to arrive. We had planned to go over a few things before the meeting."

"What things?"

Ryan laughed slightly at the remembrance. "Crowd control, I guess you could say. As silly as that sounds, we knew this meeting would be emotionally charged for some people and we wanted to have a game plan in place in case anyone..." He wasn't sure how to complete the sentence.

"Rioted?" Aidan asked.

"Got out of hand."

"Who were you worried about?" Jim stepped into the fray. "Dennis at the hospital? Bud Legaard?"

"Sure. Maybe even Val." Ryan said.

"Val Bakke?" Jim asked.

"Tor's wife?" Aidan was astonished.

"She's leading the charge on the new daycare. She wasn't

exactly happy that we were dragging our feet on giving them any money."

"And you thought that one of these individual's might get out of control?"

Ryan looked up in exasperation. "I don't know what we thought might happen. Certainly not this. But it's hard to ignore that there are people with chips on their shoulders when it comes to the city council."

Aidan made a notation in his pad. This made Ryan nervous; that nervousness might have been lessened if Ryan had known that the note Aidan jotted down was: "Pick up chips for the poker game."

"Do you think the murder is connected to Calvin's mayoral duties?" Aidan asked.

Ryan considered his answer for some time, then said, "I wouldn't presume to know something like that." It was a generic, say nothing answer truly worthy of a politician.

"Give it a shot," Aidan said in the least flippant way he could muster.

"I really can't imagine why anyone would want to kill him. Calvin Lystad was a leader, a pillar of the community. A good family man. Loved by-"

"Ryan," Jim interrupted.

"Ya," Ryan let a little of his Norwegian slip out.

"This'll go a lot faster if you stop pretending you thought Calvin was a saint."

Ryan exhaled heavily. "My mom raised me never to speak ill of the dead."

Jim gave his friend an encouraging grin but said nothing.

"Calvin Lystad was a horse's ass," Ryan said at last. "Pure and simple. He made a lot of enemies as mayor."

Aidan said, "You're a politician. You know, sometimes politicians have to make unpopular decisions."

"Yes, if they're in the best interest of the city. Calvin didn't think that way. He was an opportunist."

"How so?"

"Hmm...Like this lodging tax we instituted a few years back. He kept selling it like it was some sort of insurance policy for when the bottom fell out on the oil boom."

"It wasn't?"

"He thought if we boosted the city's budget, the council could give ourselves raises."

Aidan went back to his notebook, this time writing down what Ryan had said.

"And..."

"What, Ryan?" Jim encouraged.

"I think Cal was after people's land."

"Whose?"

"Not sure. You know, he convinced us to take that land from Bud to put in that road. Eminent domain. Why, I don't know of such a thing ever happening before in the whole history of Kirby. He hinted that that was only the beginning."

"What did he say exactly?" Aidan asked.

"I can't even remember. Nothing so straightforward as such. But I definitely had the feeling that he was going to use city funds, and eminent domain, to make some sort of land grab."

Aidan rubbed his temple. "Let's switch gears. Tell me about Wednesday night at the theater."

Jim didn't like the change of topic. He thought they were just getting somewhere. He suspected that Aidan just wanted to avoid a repeat of the discussion with Abby that had given him a headache.

Ryan started in. "As a council we decided to carry on the meeting even without the mayor. Over Lois' strong objection. Despite Calvin's absence, the meeting was going well...then again, maybe it was going well because he wasn't there."

"At what time did Calvin come into the theater?"

"I'm told it was almost 8:00. You both were there. You'd know better than me. Once the meeting started, I wasn't looking at the clock."

"It was a little before 8:00, I think," Jim said in support.

Aidan kept his focus on Ryan. "You could see a good overview of the crowd," he continued. "Did anyone leave the room at any point during the meeting?"

"Yes."

"Who?"

"Several people left and came back during the course of the meeting. Folks going to the bathroom."

"And you don't remember who any of them were?" Aidan asked.

"It didn't occur to me to keep track at the time." A spark ran across Ryan's eyes. "Mel Throntveit might know."

"The theater manager," Jim said to Aidan by way of explanation.

"He might remember who he saw as they came into the lobby."

Jim shot up to attention. "Mel Throntveit was in the lobby during the meeting?"

"I think so. I never saw him come in."

Jim and Aidan exchanged a look. The look said, "That's something."

"I think that's it for now," Aidan said. "Thank you for your time, Councilman Peterson."

Aidan rose and Jim followed suit.

"Not at all. Any way I can be of service." Ryan rose to shake both men's hands – something that Jim found odd; over the course of three years of friendship, he couldn't remember them ever shaking hands before. When both men were near the door, Ryan spoke again. "You might want to talk to the Ardises."

Aidan turned back to the councilman. "Pardon?"

"Ardis Knutson and Ardis Knudsvig. They were sitting close to where Calvin fell. If he said anything, they might have heard."

"Thank you."

"What do you think?" Aidan asked when they hit the street again.

"I think we have some people to talk to."

"The Ardises. And Mel Cronkite."

"Throntveit."

"Whatever." Aidan said, as the two started for the squad car.

"And Tor Bakke's wife."

"Yeah, I'm looking forward to that conversation. Hey sheriff, mind if I interrogate your wife for the murder of Calvin Lystad."

Jim chuckled, then ceased when he saw that Aidan was reaching for the passenger door. "What are you doing?"

Aidan tossed the keys to Jim. "I'm tired. You drive for a while."

"I can't drive a law enforcement vehicle."

Aidan got into the car. He said something, but Jim couldn't hear it from outside the vehicle. Reluctantly, he opened the front door and leaned in. "What did you say?"

"I said, 'It's not like you need a retina verification before the thing'll start.' Get in, you look foolish with your butt sticking in the air."

Jim got behind the wheel of the car. He still had no intention of driving it, but he was worried that he might indeed look foolish. Dakotans don't like to draw attention to themselves. "One other thing," Jim said.

"Start the car up," Aidan instructed, then laid back in the passenger seat as if to take a nap.

"I really don't feel comfortable driving this thing."

"Fine. But can we at least get some heat going? It may be fall for you, but it's winter for me."

Jim turned the key in the ignition. The two men sat in silence.

"Now what?" Jim asked.

"You had one more thing."

"Ya. I do remember one person who left to go to the bathroom."

Aidan perked up. "Who?"

"Ryan. He ran into the lobby just before he started the meeting. Around 7:45."

"That's a long time for Calvin to sit in the wings and bleed out."

"Yeah, I guess you're right. Where to now?" Jim asked

"Nowhere, I thought."

"Okay. Okay. I'll drive. But I am doing this against my will."

"Duly noted. I think we should talk to the theater manager first."

Jim shook his head. "Oh no. We go wherever the driver takes us."

"Fine. Does the passenger get to know where that is?"

"East Park." Jim pulled out of the space.

"East Park," Aidan repeated. "We're going to have a picnic? It is a lovely day for it."

"East Park is not a where. East Park is a who."

18

South Korea native East Park's name at birth was Dong-Min Park. . . well, technically, it was a bunch of lines that would look like gibberish to most North Dakotans. Dong-Min Park was the English equivalent of those squiggly lines. When Dr. Park moved to the United States, he wanted to sound more like an American. But instead of adopting a nice American boy's name, like Kevin or John or Verner; he decided to simply translate his given name. So his North Dakota driver's license reads "East Cleverness Park." Had his English been better when he first arrived, he may have elected a name for himself that sounded less like a summer camp for kids training for the academic decathlon.

East Park worked as a PA – physician's assistant – at St. Eustace's Hospital. In his own country, Dong-Min had been a doctor; but those credentials didn't carry the same weight in the United States. Still, North Dakota was in such desperate need for qualified health care professionals, that East made a nice wage even as a PA. More than the money though, East had come for the experience. Even as a young child, Dong-Min Park craved adventure and excitement. And when you come from halfway across the world and don't know any better, even North Dakota can seem like a land of adventure and excitement.

East Park turned out to be an elusive figure for the investigators to track down. Jim drove the sheriff's vehicle to the hospital. There they were informed that East worked the 3 pm to 11 pm shift. Aidan asked the head nurse for Park's home address. "He lives in the old Oppegaard house. The white house. Right across the street from Betty Lindstrom." In a small town, directions rarely include street names and numbers; thankfully Jim knew the house in question. When they arrived at the old Oppegaard house, East's lovely wife Honor informed them that he was out running errands. One of his stops would be a workout at the Healthy Heart Gym behind the drugstore. The men decided to meet up with him there.

East was there when the men arrived. The slight man was running full bore on one of the gym's three treadmills. "How are you, Jim?" East asked, his voice virtually unaffected by the strenuous run.

"Hoping the weather holds up for a while. East, this is Deputy Aidan Gray."

"Hello. Deputy?" East said it like a question. Jim wondered if he thought it was Aidan's name.

"Call me Aidan."

"Good to meet you." East's voice almost disappeared over the sounds of the gym machinery and East's own footsteps on the treadmill. East had a tendency to speak softly anyway. Perhaps a lingering insecurity over his English, Jim suspected. It was a needless worry. Sure East mispronounced a word here or there, and sometimes a word would escape him entirely; but the man had made great progress in the five years since moving to the United States. When he first arrived, East's accent was so thick none of the Kirbyites could understand a word he said. And vice versa.

"Can you turn off the treadmill for a moment while we ask you a few questions?" Aidan asked.

"Right in the middle of my workout?" East replied.

"It will only take a moment," Jim assured him. "Then we'll get out of your hair."

The look on East's face told Jim that he didn't quite understand what "get out of your hair" meant.

"It's not healthy to stop from a full run. I turn it down." East adjusted the dial. The full run went down to a high speed walk.

Jim and Aidan jumped onto the treadmills flanking East.

Aidan turned his on and started walking in step with East. Jim did not turn his treadmill on, but instead stood sideways to face East directly.

"East, were you working at the hospital on Wednesday night?" Aidan asked.

"Oh yes, Monday through Friday, 3:00 to 11:00." East said.

"Do you remember seeing Dennis Anderson that night while you were on your shift?"

Jim noticed a change in East. It was small, and would have been imperceptible to Aidan who was only looking in East's direction periodically. A darkening of the face, a momentary stepping out of pace. As quickly as it arrived, it was gone again.

"Yes, Mr. Anderson. I was on break. 7:50. I popped my head into his office. He was playing game on his computer. I asked what he was still doing at the hospital. He said he was going to sleep in his office. Driving in bad weather, he did not want to risk it."

"Did you see him at any other point that night?" Aidan asked.

"No."

"You worked till eleven," Jim stepped in, "so you were still there when they brought the mayor in?"

East bowed his head slightly. "Yes, so sad. Nothing we could do. He was already dead."

"East, after all of the commotion of trying to save the mayor died down, why didn't you go back and get Dennis?" Jim asked.

"I...I don't know. I did not think to."

Aidan's cell rang. He took a look at the screen and said, "I should take this." He headed outside. East seemed to relax a bit at Aidan's departure.

Jim leaned in closer to talk to East. The move was not to ensure privacy – they were the only ones in the gym at the moment – he did it for the intimidation factor. It seemed like something Kojak would do. "I don't think I've ever heard you use the phrase 'popped in' before, East."

"What that?" East asked, still walking and looking straight ahead.

"You said earlier that you popped your head into Dennis' office on Wednesday night."

"Ah, I did...Becoming more American every day, I guess." East tried to dismiss it with a smile.

"Funny thing is, when I talked to Dennis, he said the same thing. That you 'popped your head into his office.'"

"Funny thing," East agreed less than comfortably.

"Ya. You both also said that Dennis 'didn't want to risk it'."

East kept on walking. Jim reached over and pulled the red emergency stopper from East's treadmill. It wound down to a stop. East reluctantly turned his eyes to Jim.

"Why did Dennis tell you to say that?"

"I don't know what...please Jim, I don't want trouble."

"East, did you actually see Dennis on Wednesday?" Jim's voice was forceful. He was pushing; he needed to settle this while it was just the two of them.

"Yes," East answered. There was a pause. "At 5:30. When he was leaving the hospital."

"Where did he go?"

"I don't know."

"Why did he ask you to cover for him?"

"I was scared," East said, answering a question in his own head rather than Jim's. "I went along. I don't want to lose work visa. This is my home."

East turned the dial on his treadmill up. He was back to a full run. Jim thought about the fact that some people exercise in stressful situations. Nothing in the world could be more unnatural in Jim's eyes.

"Did I miss anything?" Aidan had returned.

Jim pulled back from East and turned toward Aidan with a smile. "No, not really. I think we have everything we need. Enjoy the rest of your workout, East."

19

"I feel like I walked in on something," Aidan said when they were back in the car, Jim again behind the wheel.

"It was nothing."

Aidan touched his friend's arm to get Jim to face him.

"It was nothing," he repeated. "Really."

"Well, if it turns into something, let me in on it, all right?"

The two men sat for a minute in silence.

"Let me ask you something," Jim broke the silence. "The other night. How did you know about Claudette?"

"Who?"

"My wife. How did you know she left me?"

"It was just a guess." Aidan was obviously uncomfortable.

"No. It was detective work. I think. I want to understand how you do it." Another silence. "Please."

Aidan kept his eyes glued to the road as if he were driving on the 405 freeway in Los Angeles during rush hour rather than sitting in the passenger seat of a parked car three miles north of the middle of nowhere. "I've known you for about a month now," Aidan said. "In that time, you've lost a good eight to ten pounds. Weight loss that rapid is either a crash diet, an illness or a major source of stress. I was betting on the third one. Also, you don't mention your wife much. It goes to reason that it might be because you don't want to get too deep into a discussion about her. So, I suspected something was up. My suspicions were confirmed when I saw the credit card statements lying on your desk."

"You looked through my bills?"

"I just noticed them was all. I'm a sheriff's deputy; that's what I do. I didn't look at your purchases or anything. I just saw that last month's bill was addressed to both of you and the current statement to only you"

Jim buried his head in his hands.

Aidan said, "Jim, I'm not going to tell a soul what I know."

"No, it's not that." Jim looked. "I'm in over my head here. You're right; I'm no investigator. I wouldn't know a clue if it bit me. I shouldn't be doing this. I'm not helping this case. I'm impeding it."

The men sat in silence for a while.

"So what? It doesn't matter," Aidan finally declared. "So you're clueless about clues. So you couldn't find evidence if it had a tag labeled 'evidence' attached. So you don't know your ass from a hole in the ground."

"Stop encouraging me."

"You know people. You know these people, Jim. They talk to you. And you hear them. What they're saying and what they're not saying."

"Thanks," Jim gave a wan smile.

"I need you on this. I can't finish this thing alone."

"This has gotten way too serious."

Aidan placed a hand on Jim's shoulder. "Save me, Jim Rosdahl. You're my only hope."

"Is that from a movie or something?"

"Are you kidding me?" Aidan didn't wait for an answer. "That call back at the gym was from the cops in Williston. Williams County medical examiner is performing the autopsy now."

"That's fast. Isn't it?"

"I asked them to make it their priority number one."

"And they're doing it anyway?" Jim smiled.

"I am very charming."

The ring of a cell phone filled the car before the properly sarcastic response could be formulated. This time it was Jim's phone.

"Hi, mom."

There was a sigh on the other end. "I'm over at the Good Sam. It's Doc Haugenoe's birthday." Gladys said, her everyday sternness replaced by a heavy perturbedness.

"Oh that's right, it's today, isn't it?" Silence. Jim had the distinct feeling that he was in trouble, but his mom wasn't going to lay out the reason. Jim had to go fishing. "One hundred years old. Uff da!" Silence. "Are there a lot of people there?"

"Ya. The whole town about. Everybody but *The Crier*."

"Brian's stopping down to take photos and..." Jim trailed off as he came to realize that he was probably lying.

"I have to cut the cake." She hung up.

Jim pocketed his phone. "Everything all right?"

Jim shrugged. "Sure. Fine."

"What's our next stop?" Aidan asked. "The theater manager? Sheriff's wife? Those two old ladies?"

Jim took a deep sigh and fastened his seat belt. Devoid of enthusiasm, he said, "I have to go to a birthday party."

Dr. Jeremiah "Doc" Haugenoe was celebrating his 100th birthday. Like many centenarians, "celebrating" entailed sitting in his wheelchair in the activities room of the nursing home, while people periodically leaned down to make sure he was still alive before yelling into his ear, "Happy Birthday," "How's it feel to be a hundred?" or "Do you need to go to the bathroom?"

Edith Andrist – who, when she wasn't baking inedible pies down at the senior center, worked as the Activities' Director at the Good Samaritan Nursing Home – had decorated the room quite nicely considering the budget she had to work with. Festive tablecloths, cheerful "Happy Birthday" paper centerpieces, plenty of balloons taped high enough that they wouldn't be accidentally run over by a wheelchair causing a loud pop that would wake the barely living.

Jim arrived with camera in hand, Aidan in tow. Aidan objected to coming. "I don't even know this guy."

"It's an open house," Jim insisted. "The whole community is invited."

And it appeared that the whole community had come out. It was one of those come and go affairs that are all the rage in Kirby, so there was a steady stream of folks coming and folks going. Jim walked around the room, snapping photos of the celebration's attendees, of the guest of honor, and of the ample spread. The table was loaded down with a number of Scandinavian treats – lefse, krumkake, and sandbakkels – as well as plenty of bars.

"My goodness. Did you make all of this, Edith?" Gladys Rosdahl asked with trepidation, holding an empty plate over the dessert buffet.

"No. Didn't have the time," Edith sighed. "These were all brought in by other folks."

Gladys loaded up her plate. "That's a shame," she said. "You're such a baker."

Jim came in closer to get some more shots of the birthday boy.

"Stop that." Doc Haugenoe demanded. Over the years, the volume had left the good doctor's voice, but the contrariness had remained intact.

Jim obliged. He leaned into Doc's ear.

"Happy Birthday, Doc."

The old man grunted. Jim was undaunted. "That cake looks delicious. Can I get you a slice?"

"I haven't eaten a piece of solid food in nine years," the Doc grunted. "Who are you?"

"Jim. Jim Rosdahl. Don't you remember? I'm Marlin and Gladys Rosdahl's son."

"Uff da. Don't be stupid. I'm not senile. I just couldn't see who you were. My eyeballs are a hundred years old."

"Yes, sir."

"Marlin's dead," Doc said, as if it were a pronouncement,

but Jim recognized it for the question that it was. Jim decided to settle into the chair on Doc's right. Better than bending over like an idiot with his butt hanging out.

"Yes, sir. Dad died in '93." Jim had found that with thirty-somethings, you had to use phrases like "passed away" or "went to a better place" but with old people you could speak with more bluntness about death. "Brain aneurysm."

"I knew it would be sudden. Always told him that. He was a good man."

Aidan approached. "Doc," Jim yelled. "This is Aidan Gray."

Reluctantly, he leaned in to shout into the man's ear. "Nice to meet you. Happy Birthday."

"Who are you?" Doc asked.

"Aidan Gray."

"Who?"

"Aidan Gray."

"Who?"

"Aidan Gray." Aidan looked to Jim. There was a discomfort on his face that said, "Is this really happening?" Jim smiled at the comedy unfolding. Aidan's problem was that he was misinterpreting the question. He thought the old man was asking for his name; but in North Dakota, "who are you?" means "who are your people, how would I know you?"

Jim leaned in. "Aidan just moved to Kirby last month."

"You make me nervous. Sit down."

Aidan followed his orders, taking the chair on Doc's left.

"Doc Haugenoe used to be the only doctor in the area." Jim was speaking to Aidan, but talking loud enough that the old man could be included.

Doc said, "Traveling doctor. Started during the Depression. I knew every man, woman, and child in three counties."

Aidan felt the need to respond. He said, "Wow."

"What?" Doc demanded.

"Wow," Aidan repeated, wishing he hadn't said anything to begin with.

"You a doctor?"

"No," Jim answered for him, as if Aidan required an old man interpreter, "Aidan is a deputy with the Sheriff's Office."

Doc perked up at this, as much as a 100 year-old man in a wheelchair and off solid foods can perk up. "I heard the Lystad boy got murdered."

"Yes, sir." Jim supposed that if you lived a century, you could refer to a 67 year-old man as a "boy."

Doc leaned toward Aidan. "Are you on that case?" Aidan nodded, but the man's ancient eyeballs missed it. "What?"

"He is," Aidan's interpreter shouted.

Doc Haugenoe chewed on an idea for a moment – well, gummed on it. "That youngest one was evil. Like his father. Ollie. Ole."

"Ole."

"Other two took after Mabel. She wasn't evil. Just crazy." Doc made some strange sputtering noises and shook slightly. Jim figured this was probably laughter. Once it died down, the old man continued. "Crazy. She spent a whole year, never got out of bed."

"I heard she had rheumatic fever."

The Doc sputtered and shook some more. "Rheumatic fever. I forgot that part. Nonsense."

"What did she have?"

"Ollie. Ole called me to the farm to check on her. Looked her over top to bottom. I told them she had lethargy, now."

"Lethargy?" Aidan asked.

"She was depressed," Jim interpreted.

"Ya. Depression they call it now. Lethargy. Called me a quack. So she diagnosed herself. Rheumatic fever." The Doc shook like an old car with engine trouble. "Crazy."

"Can we go now?" Aidan said softly so the old man wouldn't hear. Jim nodded. They made their loud goodbyes. As they walked away, the Ardises came up to Doc.

"Happy Birthday, Doc," Ardis Knutson said.

"Who's that?"

"Ardis Knutson."

"Who?"

"Ardis Knutson?"

"Who's that with you?"

"What?"

"Earth to Jim Rosdahl," Aidan said as he loaded something that looked like a tortilla but the locals called "lefse" onto his plate. "Where are you?"

"I'm here." Jim was at the dessert table with Aidan but his mind was definitely somewhere else.

"You know who did it," Aidan said as a matter of fact.

"No," Jim said. Not convincingly, if his friend's facial expression was any indication. "Really, I don't. Just trying to work out some things."

"You'll let me know when you do."

Aidan's phone rang. He excused himself just as Ardis Knutson and Ardis Knudsvig finished their Abbott and Costello routine with Doc Haugenoe and came to the table.

"Uff da! One hundred is too long to live," Ardis Knutson was saying as Jim came up.

"Oh hello, Jim," Ardis Knudsvig flirted subtly. "Isn't this a nice reception? The bars look so good."

"Did Edith make this?" Ardis Knutson asked.

"No, I don't believe so," Jim said.

"Good."

"Have either of you ladies heard when the service for Calvin Lystad is going to be held?" Jim asked. The chip fell off of Ardis Knutson's shoulder, while the other Ardis' smile grew. If you want to make friends with a Dakotan, ask them if they know something you don't.

"Hazel had hoped to have it this weekend," Ardis Knudsvig started, "but there are problems."

"What problems?"

"Calvin's brother and some of the extended family can't make it here that soon. And also there's. . ." her voice trailed off.

"The autopsy." Often, Ardis Knutson rushed in where Ardis Knudsvig feared to tread. "Hazel can't have the body until it's over. And who knows when that will be?"

"It's all just such a shame," Ardis Knudsvig lamented, shaking her head. Whether she was referring to the logistics of the funeral or the fact that someone had been murdered or just death in general or something else entirely was unclear to the other two.

"Ya," Ardis Knutson agreed. Jim nodded.

"You know, I'll never forget being in that theater and seeing that red stain on Calvin's shirt. Watching him fall to the ground." Jim said. "Consider yourselves lucky you weren't there."

"But we were there," Ardis Knudsvig was excited to let Jim know.

"Couldn't have been closer," the older, crankier Ardis said, "He nearly fell on me."

"Really?" Jim acted surprised, and worried he wasn't a very good actor.

"Ya."

"Ya."

Jim leaned in, as if in confidence. "Can I ask you a question?" He whispered to reinforce the clandestine aura he was going for. Ardis Knudsvig nodded. Ardis Knutson said "ya" softly, because she wasn't very good at moving her neck.

"Did either of you hear Calvin say anything?" The women's eyes grew large. "I feel like I almost heard him say something; but I was way up front." Jim shook the thought away. "Probably just my imagination."

"No, he did say something."

"Ya. He did."

"What?" Jim asked.

Ardis Knutson grabbed Jim's wrist and pulled him in closer. The other Ardis rolled her eyes preemptively. Ardis Knutson said, "Right before he fell, he looked at me. Almost pleadingly. And he said, 'in my body'."

"In my body?" Jim asked.

"Dear. We've been over this," came Ardis Knudsvig, "What he said was 'I'm not Bobby'."

Ardis Knutson snorted at this. She rotated to face her best friend. "That's stupid. It doesn't make sense?"

"It makes as much sense as 'in my body'."

"Why would he say he's not Bobby?"

"Well, he wasn't Bobby, was he then? Why would he say 'in my body'?"

"He was telling me that the bullet was still in his body."

Jim interjected. "He wasn't shot." The comment didn't seem to register with either Ardis.

"I was closer," Ardis Knutson continued. "I could hear him better."

"But your ears are worse than mine."

"What?"

"He said 'I'm not Bobby.' He was dying. Delirious. He might have been hallucinating."

"Too bad he fell when he did. He would have given us a whole list of names of the people he wasn't."

"You have a good day, ladies," Jim said as he backed away.

Jim found Aidan in the parking lot, with his phone to his ear, nodding and saying "Yes" a lot. When Aidan saw Jim, he put the phone in his pocket.

"That's an abrupt way to end a call." Jim pointed out.

"I've been off the phone for five minutes. I just didn't want to go back inside. We all done here?"

Jim nodded. The two men walked toward the squad car.

"That call. . . William Legaard didn't go to Arizona."

"Bud Legaard," Jim corrected. "He didn't?"

"Not as far as I can figure. He didn't fly out of Minot or Williston. And his cars are just sitting in the driveway of his house. Haven't been able to contact him at home. Either home."

"Then where is he, then?"

"That's a very good question." Aidan walked over to the driver's side of the car.

"I'm not driving anymore?" Jim asked.

"I'm afraid of where you might take me next." Aidan opened the door, stopped and looked over at Jim. "I saw you talking to the Ardises. So, what did Calvin say before he died?"

"Nothing I can repeat."

20

Aidan dropped Jim off at the newspaper office. Jim was tired and he wanted to be alone, but he didn't feel like he should go home. He had neglected his work at the newspaper the past few days, and he had quite a bit of catching up to do. It was just before 5:00. The staff usually work until 5:30 but Jim told Toni and Layla that they could go home and start the weekend early.

After they left, Jim went into his tiny office. Resting on his keyboard was a note: "Working on water plant story. You'll need to cover Doc's thing. -Bri". Jim balled the note up and threw it in his waste basket. Although he wanted to scream, he decided not to; it wouldn't be dignified. But he was still a ball of frustration.

It wasn't just Brian's incompetence that was upsetting him. Jim was mad at himself too. Though he would be loath to admit it, when this whole "investigation" began, Jim was delighted about it. As Aidan had suggested earlier, Jim did feel like one of those amateur detectives in those mystery stories that Claudette (and Jim too sometimes) loved so much. Miss Marple nabbing murderers from her cozy little cottage. Father Brown solving crimes in between Masses.

But his visit with Doc Haugenoe had reminded Jim that Calvin Lystad was a real person, with a family and a history. That realization disturbed him. Calvin Lystad had enemies. He had ill-wishers. But he also had friends; he had family. Calvin Lystad was a bundle of virtue and vice, charity and contempt, saint and sinner. Just like every man. The ending of a human life should give one pause at the very least; not provide delight. Calvin Lystad had lived 67 years on this planet. That's a drop in the bucket of time, but every drop matters. Every life lost should be mourned.

Jim was full. His brain was full of facts and opinion. His heart was full of emotion. His liver was full of bile. Other parts were full of other things. He couldn't take another drop. Maybe a scream was the only way to let some of it out. He was alone. No one to hear him or judge him. This is it, Jim decided, I'm going to scream.

"Hello," came a voice from the front. "Jim, you back there?"

Saved from himself, Jim came out of the office to see Candy Gillund standing at the front. She had placed a small package on the counter.

"Hi, Candy. What can I do for you?"

"You got a package. I'm not in the habit of delivering, but I thought you might want it today." Candy ran her finger along the address label. "It's from Claudette."

Jim's face was unchanged. "Thanks. That was kind of you. I could have picked it up in the morning." Jim took up the box.

Slightly deflated, Candy said goodbye and headed back to the door. Then, in an attempt to redeem the visit, she turned back and said, "I don't suppose you've heard the latest. It turns out that before he died, the mayor had been carrying on an illicit affair for several years."

"I hate to break it to you, but I've talked to Abby. There was nothing going on there."

"Everybody knows that." Candy rolled her eyes, as if Jim had just said "Milk comes from cows." It was funny how quickly what everybody knows changes. "It wasn't Abby he was carrying on with."

"Who then?"

The postmaster's eyes gleamed with delight as she revealed, "Lois Pedersen."

21

"The mayor died of poisoning!?" Jim nearly dropped the phone.

"No, I'm still pretty sure it was the blade through the heart that killed him," came Aidan's voice from the other end. "But he was definitely poisoned first."

Jim surveyed the contents of his office, and felt like he didn't recognize a thing. He looked at the box from Claudette – now opened – that Candy had delivered just moments ago. He played with the cord on his office phone, a nervous habit. He did this even though he was speaking on his cell.

"Who...Did the same person poison and stab him?" Jim asked.

"Wasn't there."

"What was it?"

"The poison?" Aidan asked. There was a pause and Jim could hear the shuffling of papers on Aidan's end. "A cocktail of lye and oxalic acid, a poison found in rheum rhabarbarum."

"Is there an English version of that?"

"Rhubarb."

"Rhubarb?"

"You know, that stuff you tried to make me eat when I first moved here." Aidan said. "Apparently, the stalks are okay for human consumption but the leaves are poisonous."

"Sure," Jim said. That was common knowledge around these parts. "You sure it wasn't accidental poisoning? Everything's poisonous if you ingest too much of it. Water can be poisonous."

"The rhubarb perhaps. But people generally don't go around intentionally ingesting lye."

"Well." Jim dragged out the word. He raised an eyebrow and nodded his head from side to side. "Some of us do."

"What?"

"Lye is used to make lutefisk."

"What the hell is loonafist?"

Jim explained what lutefisk was, it's preparation, and it's iconic status in Norwegian culture. Aidan was appalled. Jim tried, in vain, to explain the subtle joys of Scandinavian cuisine. Aidan made a gagging sound then asked if they could change the subject.

Jim invited Aidan to come along with him to the football game at the high school that night. Aidan declined.

"Oh, come on," Jim insisted. "The Majestics are undefeated."

"The Majestics? The Majestic What?"

"The Clark County Majestics. That's it."

"You can't have an adjective as a mascot. That's like if Notre Dame were just the Fighting."

"Game starts at 7:30."

"It's like picking a color and saying 'that's my mascot'. You wouldn't have maroon as your mascot."

"The Cleveland Browns? The Cincinnati Reds?"

Aidan paused. "Yeah, but that's Ohio."

"I'll be at the game tonight. You're welcome to meet me there."

"You know what this business with the poison means, don't you?" Aidan asked. He had no interest in the game.

"What?"

"Poison would have made Calvin pretty weak. In which case, I figure just about anyone in this town but Doc Haugenoe could have stabbed him."

Aside

What exactly is lutefisk?

Lutefisk is a stinky, gelatinous mound that was once fish. Lutefisk is a Norwegian delicacy. Delicacy is defined as "there isn't enough money on the planet to pay someone to eat it more than once a year." As a general rule, everyone hates lutefisk but they'll eat it once each winter for the sake of tradition. There is a small contingent of people who actually like lutefisk; but even they hate lutefisk.

Traditionally prepared, lutefisk takes between 10 and 14 days to make. This ordeal begins with a salted, dried cod which is soaked in cold water for four to six days. After this, the cod spends two days in a cold lye bath, followed by another four to six days in cold water. The resulting mass is then covered in salt to remove moisture, then rinsed to remove salt, then steamed or boiled to remove any remaining taste. The fact that this process is ever undertaken and that the finished product is ever consumed is proof that Norwegians have a great sense of humor.

22

The sun went down. Jim killed all the lights in the *Crier* building save for his desk lamp. He sat at his desk. He studied his left hand as he rotated it – palm side up, palm side down, repeat. On his fourth finger was his wedding ring. The ring he had bought almost thirty years ago. The ring that he had purchased "on time" (as they used to call credit). The ring Claudette had placed on his finger and pledged to him before their family, before their pastor and before God, that she would be faithful to the end.

On the finger next to it – his pinky – was another ring. A little loose. Claudette's ring. The one he had placed on her finger before God, et al. On his desk lay a jewelry box – the original one the rings had come in. (Claudette was sentimental about some things.) Beside the jewelry box was the package, now empty, that Kirby's postmaster had delivered an hour earlier.

Friday night. Clark County High School. Knute Rosdahl Field.

In the end, Jim was relieved to go to the game alone. The last few days – well, months really – had been exhausting. He looked forward to a relaxing night – no family drama, no murder investigation. There was only one hitch in Jim's plan: He lived in a small town. In a small town, you go to church with the people you work with. In a small town, you see at the grocery store the people you just bad-mouthed at the barbershop. In a small town, you attend football games with the people you're investigating for murder.

Jim went to buy his ticket and found that he was in line behind Abby Quicke and her husband Hank. The three had a pleasant conversation about the weather – *They say there's going to be another snowstorm on Monday* – and didn't discuss anything else. As he passed the concession stand, Jim exchanged hellos with Ryan Peterson. Nothing more. Moving up the bleachers, he shared a quick word with about a half dozen people before opting to sit alone in the upper corner. Those he bypassed would have been reluctant to admit their relief.

The game started with the Tigers receiving. A minute into the quarter, though, the Majestics' own Gage Oien knocked the ball out of the hands of the Tigers' running back. Junior Keaton Thingvold recovered, and ran the ball in for a touchdown. Jett Stromstad made an effortless kick for the extra point. It was looking good for an undefeated season for the Majestics. Jim applauded with the rest of the fans – a respectable Dakotan clap, nothing too ostentatious. Jim was smiling like the other fans, but not because of the play. *Gage? Keaton? Jett?* Jim thought, What are parents doing to their children? What happened to good solid normal names? He looked over at the old guard, elderly men who never missed a game. Verner. Lars. Harlan. Knute. *Good solid, normal names.*

Dennis Anderson walked past the old guard. Jim followed Dennis' movement with his eyes. Dennis headed over to the snack bar. Jim stood and made a step toward the aisle – never taking his eyes off of Dennis. A couple got in line behind him, and Jim decided to go back to his seat.

At the end of the second quarter, the Majestics were up 32 to 6. As the teams made their way off the field at halftime, the crowds poured out of the bleachers. The temperature was in the high twenties, but the wind made it feel colder than that. It was time to stand up, walk around, and try to warm up.

Jim stood but stayed up in the bleachers and watched the two hundred of so fans below. Parents, high school students, community supporters, neighbors, friends. He looked around and realized that the Pedersens were not in attendance this evening. Arley and Lois Pedersen hadn't had a child in high school for at least fifteen years, but they still came to every game. Even the week Arley was at St. Eustace recovering from kidney stones, the hospital gave the okay for him to be taken to the game in the ambulance. They backed the thing right onto the running track surrounding the field, opened the door, and Arley watched from his stretcher. (*You probably couldn't get away with that sort of thing in Chicago*, Jim thought.) The Pedersens did not miss games. Until now. The news, or the rumor – what's the difference? – circulating about the mayor carrying on with his city clerk had made the rounds by now. That was too much to face. You couldn't go to a game and look your neighbors in the eye and exchange pleasant hellos and chat about the weather.

Things had changed. Someone had introduced murder into this close-knit community. And that murder had brought other changes. The Pedersens missing football games. Jim sitting alone when there were friends all around. North Dakotans don't like change. (They still call the Farmers Fidelity Insurance office the Penney Building, for goodness sake.) This murderer was bringing a lot of change.

A thought came to Jim like a bolt of lightning. In the end this investigation would require him to make a choice between telling the truth and keeping things the way they are. He didn't know what that meant exactly, but he could feel the truth of it nonetheless. Jim decided to chock it up to a wild thought, rather than insight.

As the halftime clock worked its way down to zero, the fans returned to the bleachers. The teams returned to the field and play resumed. The second half shaped up much like the first half had. The only difference was that the audience's applause grew more tepid as the shutout become more inevitable. If you want to get a North Dakotan excited, you've got to give him some challenge at least. This game wasn't cutting it for the fans.

During the third quarter Jim noticed Dennis Anderson

again down near the field. He was making his way over to the two Porta-Johns brought out for each game. Dennis went inside one. Jim left the stands and went down to the Porta-Johns. He stood outside the one that Dennis was in and prayed that no one else would come over. Just as he gave his internal "amen," Allan Borreson got in line behind Jim. He turned and smiled at Allan.

"Good evening, Jim. That wind's something all right."

"Evening, Allan. I think that other one's empty. You go ahead."

Allan gave Jim a puzzled look. "Why don't. . ." Allan could see that Jim was not looking in his direction. "Ya. Okay." Allan disappeared behind a puke green door.

Another puke green door opened and Dennis Anderson appeared. He saw Jim, and a look of concern came upon him. "Evening, Jim." His voice was pleasant but his face made no attempt to convey it. "It's all yours."

"How about we walk and talk." Jim's request sounded a lot like a demand.

Dennis nodded and the two walked over to the school building where there wouldn't be any traffic.

"I spoke to East Park today."

The hospital administrator pulled a cigarette out of his coat pocket. "Mind?" Jim shook his head. Dennis lit up. "I expected you would. You've got to make sure everyone's stories check out."

"And yours certainly checks out. Word for word."

"That's a good thing, right?" Dennis let out a puff of smoke.

"You scripted him on what to say."

"That's the most-"

"After some pushing, East admitted that he last saw you at 5:30."

"He's lying." Dennis backed up a few steps toward the field.

"Where were you Wednesday night, Dennis?" Jim moved in step with him.

Dennis put the cigarette out on the ground even though it was still mostly intact. "I was at the hospital all night."

"Where were you?"

"I'm telling you."

"Where were you?" Jim asked. He was shaking with rage. Dennis looked in terror at Jim's eyes.

"Okay, okay. I was home."

"You're lying. You weren't home. I talked to your neighbors. They didn't see your car." Now it was Jim who was lying.

"I swear to you, I didn't kill Calvin. Please don't hit me Jim."

Jim realized that he was holding onto the collar of Dennis' coat with his left hand; his right hand was balled into a raised fist and pulled back ready to strike. He was not certain how long he had been in this position. Jim recovered some of his sense and lowered his hand, though it remained in a fist.

"I know you didn't kill him."

"You do? Then why...?"

Jim looked at the hand still holding onto Dennis' coat. His left hand. The ring on his fourth finger. The loose ring on his fifth.

"Who is it this time?"

Dennis regained enough composure to straighten up and pull Jim's hand off of his coat. "I don't like what you're insinuating."

"Whose wife is it this time?"

"It's not like that, Jim. I know we've had our issues. But that's ancient history."

"Who is she?"

"Jim, I can assure you..." Dennis lost his voice. The look on Jim's face told him it would be best if he found it again. "I'm not going to tell you her name. This is between her and me."

"That's fair enough. It's none of my business." Jim seemed to relax a bit, which put Dennis more at ease. "It's her husband's business, though. He probably has a right to know."

"Can I get back to the game now?" Dennis asked.

"Sure."

Dennis turned and made a few steps toward the field.

"Be careful, Dennis." He stopped and turned at Jim's words. "When he does find out he's liable to do something like this."

And Jim Rosdahl sent his right fist squarely into Dennis Anderson's nose. Dennis went down like a lead balloon. Like a lead balloon that was bleeding from the nose and mouth. Dennis placed his hand on his face. He pulled his hand back, and noticed blood. "Oh my God."

"No more talk about East losing his work visa. I don't want to come back and have another discussion about it."

Jim's breath was heavy as he walked back toward the field. With each heavy step, the adrenaline dissipated more and his breath moved closer to normal. By the time he returned to his seat in the bleachers, Jim Rosdahl had transformed back into a Norwegian.

The Majestics trounced the Tigers, 63-10.

23

"He says that he fell on a patch of ice walking back to his truck after the game," Arnie Lund told Lars Whalon the next morning at Kirby Auto Parts.

Verner confirmed the story. "Yep."

Lars Whalon shook his head. "Uff da."

Lars' young assistant Lee Johnson had come in on Saturday to get a jump on the inventory tracking; but he had been sucked into the conversation. "What do you mean 'he says'?"

Lee eyed Arnie. Then Verner eyed Arnie. Then Lars eyed Arnie.

"I don't mean nothing by it, now." Arnie assured them.

Silence. Verner Svangstu went back to his paper. Lars wiped the counter. Lee thought about inventory, but wasn't ready to act upon those thoughts.

"But if I did mean something by it," Arnie said, "it's that I would expect someone falls on the ice, they break an arm before they break a nose."

"Ah, you try to catch the fall," Lee explained to the other two men who already knew what Arnie meant.

"Ya," Arnie agreed.

"You think someone hit him?" Lars asked.

"I couldn't say."

"Who do you think did it?"

"Again I couldn't say."

Silence. Verner, Lars and Lee returned to their respective time-passing duties.

"But if I *were* to say, now..."

- - - -

"Jim Rosdahl."

Marsha Hedahl clucked and wagged her finger at her niece. "That boss of yours thinks he's some sort of detective now. He's making a fool of himself, is what he's doing."

Layla Hedahl gave her aunt a noncommittal smile.

"Don't quit your day job," Marsha continued with a laugh. The idea came to her suddenly that she was being a mite bit insensitive. Her manner softened. "I know you like Jim. I do too. But he's in over his head. He's getting a little puffed up, you know."

Layla often came in and worked at Jen's Yarn Barn on Saturdays. Marsha didn't really need the help – business was rarely brisk – but it did give them a chance to catch up on the doings around Kirby. This afternoon, however, Layla was regretting her decision to come in.

"I think it's the deputy who's really doing the investigating."

"Ya. How could I forget him? Looks like he's 12-years-old. Probably doesn't even shave every day. What does he know about solving a murder?"

Marsha Hedahl was like a second mother to Layla and she loved her. But she also liked Jim an awful lot. He was a gentle soul and a good boss to work for. He always gave a generous Christmas bonus. She didn't really know this deputy, but if Jim was in his court, he must be a good guy. Also, he was very handsome. For a 12-year-old.

"I suppose he knows more about it than either of us."

Marsha snorted. "I know enough not to interrogate the sheriff's wife. Those two ambushing Val right as she's washing the breakfast dishes. And Tor wasn't even around to defend her. She was about in tears when they left her."

Marsha Hedahl and Val Bakke were close friends. Layla knew in her heart that it was futile to argue with her aunt on this issue. But Layla liked futility. That's why she worked for a newspaper.

"They have to talk to everyone, I suppose. It wouldn't look right if they questioned everyone but her."

"I'm not saying she liked the mayor. They didn't exchange Christmas cards, for sure. But she and Tor were at my house having dinner that night. If Val's learned to be in two places at once, she hasn't told me. No sir." End of conversation. Marsha was done.

Layla wasn't quite on the same page. "You said they left around 6:30 because the storm was getting bad. Calvin didn't die until almost 8:00."

Marsha fell silent. The silence was deafening.

Layla turned toward the rack of blouses near the counter. "Did these just come in?"

"A few days ago." Marsha's sourness was gone in a flash.

"They are just absolutely darling."

- - - -

"Thank you."

"It's absolutely darling," Louise Granrud repeated.

"Got it over at the Yarn Barn," Margaret Stromstad said with lowered head. She never would have purchased such a flashy top if she had known it would garner so much attention.

"The Yarn Barn, you say?" Betty Lindstrom asked for clarification.

"Whose bid is it?" Eugenia Ingqvist didn't give a rip about Margaret's damned blouse. She came to the Kirby Senior Citizen Center every Saturday afternoon to play bridge, dammit. Even the Saturday when she accidentally drove her car into her garage door, Eugenia still managed to make it to bridge on time. Unfortunately, for the rest of the old biddies, the game was just an excuse to gossip. But Eugenia would take what she could get. Bridge was a dying game, it got harder every year to find people who knew how to play it.

The other widows broke off their chatter for a few minutes

to indulge Eugenia's demand for a game. (Margaret Stromstad wasn't technically a widow, but the others tried to treat
her with kindness just the same.) Eugenia's was the dummy
hand that round, so Betty wondered why she was in such a
rush in the first place. When play got underway, Eugenia wondered that too. Her partner, Louise was absolutely hopeless
when it came time for her to manage both hands on her own.
Betty and Margaret won the hand, handily.

While the cards were being shuffled for the next round,
Margaret brought up Mel Throntveit.

"He manages the theater, doesn't he?" Betty asked. Margaret nodded.

"What about him?" Louise joined in.

"He was questioned today about the murder." Margaret
said.

Louise and Betty registered their shock. Even Eugenia forgot about the game momentarily.

"Do they think he killed the mayor?" asked Betty.

"Ya." Margaret nodded. "Of course, they wouldn't come
right out and say that to him, Betty. But that's the truth of the
matter. They think Calvin was fine and dandy when he walked
into the theater on Wednesday. Mel was waiting for him in the
lobby. Stabbed him right then and there."

Eugenia grunted. Story had turned into legend. This is why
she hated gossip. "Jim would never say that."

Margaret rolled her eyes subtly. "I said he didn't come out
and say that. But that's what he thinks. Him and that cop."

"Doesn't Mel lead the singing at Immanuel?" Betty asked
even though she knew the answer full well. Immanuel was
Kirby's Lutheran Church.

"I don't see what motive Mel would have for killing the
mayor."

"He doesn't have one, Louise. But Jim gets it into his head
'Why didn't Mel see Calvin when he came into the lobby?' He
must be the killer. But Mel has that little office behind the con-

cession stand where he rests his feet when no one's buying popcorn. What they need to do is stop harassing folks around here and start looking at these oil men we got here. Some shady people, them."

"I hate to say this," Louise said shaking her head, "because Gladys is a good friend, but I think her Jim has..." and then she didn't say what she hated to say.

"He's gotten a little full of himself." Betty Lindstrom made her first declarative statement of the afternoon.

"Ya."

"Ya."

"Who's bid?" Eugenia demanded.

24

Saturday had proven to be a day of fruitless investigation for Jim and Aidan. Val Bakke had been all kinds of unhelpful when they stopped by that morning to ask a few questions. Neither Jim nor Aidan had given serious consideration to her being the murderer. Still they were curious why she hadn't gone to the city council meeting.

The exchange did not go well: Val refused to answer question one without her lawyer present, or her husband the sheriff at the very least. She insisted that – despite evidence to the contrary – she and the mayor had had an amicable professional relationship; furthermore, she barely knew Calvin outside of her dealings with the city council regarding the daycare. She continued with how greatly disappointed she was in Jim, whose parents were "good people and raised you better than to do this, going around dragging other people's names through the mud, you know." She was on the verge of tears (or perhaps screams) as she insisted the men leave. She'd been so angry she hadn't even offered them something to eat. When Jim and Adian stepped outside, Val slammed the door behind them.

At their next stop, Mel Throntveit chose not to hold back. He sobbed full out for most of the interview. He wasn't the killer, he begged them to believe. He liked Calvin. They used to go pheasant hunting together. When Aidan assured Mel that they just wanted to know what he saw that night, Mel went into another round of weeping. He went into the office after the concession line had gone down to rest his feet. He had been negligent in his duties. If he had been at the counter, maybe he would have seen who stabbed the mayor. Perhaps, the killer would have stopped when he saw Mel. Maybe, Calvin would still be alive if he had just stayed in the lobby. Mel fell apart. When it was determined that all of Aidan and all of Jim couldn't put Mel Throntveit back together again, they left and headed to Jim's house.

Jim extended a dinner invitation to Aidan. "Mom's coming over. I'm making spaghetti."

"On one condition. We don't talk about the case."

Jim agreed.

As soon as they were in his house, Aidan broke the agreement he had initiated. "The way I see it, we've got three categories here: family, politics and land. If we could just establish concretely why Calvin was killed, we could narrow down our list of suspects. What's your money on?"

"I don't want to play."

"I'm going with family. If you're going to get killed, it's usually by a family member. And it would mean that either the wife or the brother did it. Maybe the sister-in-law. Which one do you think it is?"

"This isn't a game." Jim turned on the faucet, filling a large pot with water.

"I know this isn't a game," Aidan said. "This is part of the investigation too. Considering the facts. Listening to your gut. Coming up with scenarios, what ifs." Aidan grabbed the loaf of French bread on the counter and began slicing it with the kitchen knife. "Do you not have an opinion about this?"

"I think it's about the land, okay."

"Okay," Aidan said.

The men worked in silence. Jim placed the pot on the stovetop and added some heat. He grabbed margarine from the fridge and spread it on the slices of bread that Aidan had cut.

Jim set the butter knife down and looked at his friend. "Maybe it's time that I stepped away from this thing."

"Step away from what?" The question didn't need an answer. "You can't quit now. What would Agatha Christie say?"

Aidan's teasing confirmed something for Jim. "I went into this thing like a game. But it's not. I am not qualified to do this. It's been three days now and we're no closer to finding Calvin's killer."

"It's *only* been three days. It's not exactly a cold case."

"It's time I stop running around playing Columbo."

"Who?"

"God, you're young."

"I need your help. You know these people, I don't."

Jim went into the living room and sat in his recliner. Aidan followed, but did not sit. "You're right, I do know these people. They're my neighbors, my friends. Some of them are family. I can't do this to them anymore."

"You're afraid."

"Ya. I'm afraid of what I'm doing to them with my pseudo-investigating."

"No, you're afraid of what they're doing to you." Aidan settled down onto the couch. "People are starting to judge you. Talk about you behind your back. You're worried about your reputation."

Jim considered this. "What if I am? Around here, what else have you got?"

"I think your water's boiling," Aidan said. The men went back to the kitchen and worked on dinner in silence.

Gladys Rosdahl opened the front door – Jim never locked it – without knocking. "I'm here," she announced. She entered the kitchen and saw Aidan, "Oh, hello," she said to the unexpected dinner guest in a tone that defied interpretation. After sampling the spaghetti sauce – it needed more salt – Gladys went into the dining room to set the table.

"I'll continue by myself," Aidan said when he and Jim were alone in the kitchen. "But I want to go on record as saying this is stupid."

"So noted."

"You shouldn't stop asking questions, just because you're afraid the answers might affect you personally."

Jim, his mother and Aidan enjoyed a pleasant evening. Dinner was lovely, though the spaghetti sauce was a touch salty. They talked about football. They talked about the people that Gladys had seen at the Kirby Farmer's Market that morning. They talked about Burt and Alice Thingvold's upcoming fiftieth wedding anniversary; and played the common small town game where they tried to remember the names and current whereabouts of all of the Thingvold children. They talked about the weather. They managed to not say a single word about Calvin Lystad's death or about the investigation.

It took some effort.

25

In 1971 – January 22 – Verner Svangstu got a call in the middle of the night from John Lund. A blizzard had made its way through the area. For the crew that plowed the roads in and around Kirby, it was all hands on deck. Lazarus Oien was sick in bed, could Verner step in this once and take his place?

Verner's first thought was, *Snowplow guys don't call in sick. Lazarus Oien must be on death's door.* Turned out Verner was right; Lazarus died three days later.

The second thought that went through Verner's mind was, *I've never used a snowplow before. I'm liable to do some real damage to the streets. Or to the plow. Or to myself.*

Those were his thoughts. His only words were, "Ya, sure. Just this once."

More than four decades later, Verner was still one of the snowplow guys. He was in his eighties now; it was probably time to retire, but who knew when that day would actually come. There weren't a lot of people standing in line begging for a chance to get up hours before the crack of dawn in sub-freezing temperatures and clear roadways.

It was Sunday morning and Verner sat behind the wheel of his plow, working methodically. It hadn't snowed in Kirby since the night of Calvin Lystad's murder, four days before. Still there was plenty of snow down at the fairgrounds. During the winter, these grounds served as the dump site for the literal tons of snow cleared from Kirby streets.

Verner didn't particularly like the way that snow had been placed here after Wednesday's storm. He felt it was sloppy work. You can't just dump it anywhere. Back when John Lund, Lazarus Oien and those guys were working, they planned ahead. These fairgrounds would need to hold a lot more snow before the winter was through. Hell, winter wouldn't even officially start for another two months. Another storm was supposed to be coming in that night, so Verner came down to organize the old snow and make way for the new.

After so many years, the work was mindless. But Verner was never bored; he had plenty to occupy his time. He spent the first half hour cursing the current generation who did such lazy work that forced him to come out here in the first place. They've got their heads so full of dreams and fluff, that they don't know the value of hard work anymore. This thought segued nicely into Verner's own youthful ambitions. His mind went to the air. He had always wanted to learn to fly a plane, and never had. John Lund had taken him up in his small prop plane a couple of times, had even let him take the controls. But that wasn't the same as knowing how to fly. Then his thoughts moved to his family, to his beautiful daughters. All married now. All with families of their own. Joyce in the Cities. Audrey in Washington State. Lois here in Kirby. Poor Lois, with all of this business with the mayor. It was too much for Verner's mind to process, so he decided to think about ice fishing. It was sizing up to be a good long, cold winter. Great for ice fishing. It might be time to buy some new equipment; he'd have to check and see if-.

That's when something went *sccreeeec-phpt* and the snow-plow buckled. Verner hadn't seen what he'd hit. It's not that he wasn't paying attention; whatever it was had been completely buried under snow. That kind of thing happened. You got a *sccreeeec-phpt* every now and then. Although, this was a pretty big *sccreeeec-phpt*, whatever it was.

Working on instinct, Verner stopped the plow immediately. Now he threw the thing into reverse and slowly backed away. He stared at the object for some time trying to figure out what it was, and once he did, he spent some time trying to wish it into being something else.

"Uff da!"

There in the snow lay Bud Legaard.

26

Jim woke on Sunday morning feeling refreshed, rejuvenated, and just the slightest bit guilty. This guilt was overshadowed by the huge boulder of responsibility that had been removed from his shoulders the night before. The murder investigation was behind him now. He could return to his simple life. Living in Kirby, publishing a paper, looking after his mother who was just on the precipice of needing to be looked after: these things weren't easy, but they were simple.

Jim liked life simple. And life had been too complicated lately; Claudette's leaving had seen to that. Jim didn't suppose things would return to simple there anytime soon. For the time being Jim didn't have to face her, but what would happened when his daughter-in-law finally had her baby? He would, of course, go down to Bismarck to see the kids and his new grandchild. And Claudette would be there. That would not be simple.

The murder of Calvin Lystad had made things "not simple" as well. Jim had leaped without looking, and what had his eagerness gotten him? Complications. Work at the newspaper was suffering. Friends were becoming strangers. He had turned a suspicious eye toward the people in the community he cared for most deeply. And what did all of these sacrifices produce? Nothing. He didn't know how to investigate a crime, to sift through clues, to unmask a murderer. If anything, he had potentially harmed the investigation. He hoped not. He also hoped he hadn't damaged his friendship to Aidan irrevocably.

Jim shoved all of these thoughts into a file and placed them into a cabinet in the back of his mind, hoping to not have to open it again for a while. He took a long, hot shower, humming excerpts from Beethoven's Sixth Symphony the entire time. He dressed in the suit he only brought out for weddings, funerals, Christmas, and Easter. (Today was a day of rebirth, an Easter of sorts.) He closed the door of his house without locking it, opened the door of his car which was also unlocked, turned the key that was already in the ignition, and went to pick up his mother for church.

There are three churches in Kirby. At the Kirby Assembly of God – which the Rosdahls attended – they sang some rousing old hymns and a few "modern" choruses written in the 1970s. Over at Immanuel Lutheran Church they sang even older hymns, depressing dirges that nobody but Lutherans had ever heard. Over at St. Mary Catholic Church they sang hymns old enough to put the Lutheran hymns to shame; they even threw in some light calisthenics – kneel, stand, sit, kneel, stand, repeat – for good measure.

During the communal prayer at St. Mary's it was announced that lifelong parishioner Bud Legaard had died. A prayer was then offered for Bud, his family (of which he had none), and his friends (of which he had even fewer). At Immanuel Lutheran the news was delivered more sinisterly during the morning announcements when someone from the congregation informed everyone that "another body has turned up." Apparently, no one at the Kirby Assembly of God was on the inside track of local news that morning, so the worshipers there did not learn of Bud's passing. They had to be content with merely the Father, the Son and the Holy Ghost.

After church Jim ate lunch with Gladys – who ate dinner – back at her house. It was a simple meal of salad and Gladys' potato soup (by far the least successful dish in her repertoire). They had strawberries and cream for dessert. Following the meal, they settled in the living room to watch an episode of *Little House on the Prairie* on cable. It was in the middle of a heated argument between Laura Ingalls and Nellie Olson that Jim decided to head across the alley to *The Crier* and get a little work done.

There Jim wrote a story about Doc Haugenoe's one-hundredth birthday celebration. It was a nice little piece about the party, with quotes from the staff and some of the other residents at the Good Sam. He even managed to find two quotes from Doc himself that weren't too ornery for print. He sorted through the many pictures he'd taken at the party and selected four to run with the story. The finished product seemed a paltry acknowledgment for surviving 100 years on this planet, so Jim decided to add a sidebar story. He wrote a short biography of Doc's life, focusing on a medical practice that spanned 55 years, serving thousands of people in three counties: treating their illnesses, mending their wounds, and even delivering the occasional baby (though many women gave birth at home without aid of physician back in Doc's day).

With that story done, Jim decided to tackle the murder story. Get it over with. Although Calvin's death seemed like a year ago, it had been less than a week. This would be the first issue of the newspaper to mention it. Jim did his reporter duty: laying out the who, what, when, where, and how of the city council meeting for all the readers who would already know them. Jim steered clear of the "why." That wasn't his job anymore. He threw in a couple of generic quotes from Deputy Gray about the ongoing investigation into Calvin's murder. Thankfully, Jim had gotten these from Aidan before their recent unpleasantness.

Jim finished the story and then, fighting every instinct he had, emailed a copy to Sheriff Tor Bakke. They had made a deal: Jim could work on the case and Tor would have story approval. Jim imagined his father Marlin spinning in his grave. Jim thought it was a bad idea at the time and now he knew it. He had compromised his journalistic integrity for the opportunity to play detective, an effort that had been for naught. But it would only be this once, Jim reminded himself. Future stories would require no editorial approval from the sheriff.

Jim's backing out of the investigation had nullified the contract; it was only logical. Jim wondered if his "cousin" Tor would subscribe to the same brand of logic.

The sun was low in the sky when Jim finished his work. Clouds were moving in from the north, but the Sunday night storm was still hours away. Jim decided to go for a walk while the weather was still nice – 27 degrees with five mile-an-hour winds being considered "nice weather" by North Dakota standards. He walked for a half hour through the mostly residential streets of Kirby. In that time, he encountered a few dozen cars on the road. Jim lifted his hand in acknowledgment. If the driver was a local and paying attention, he or she would wave back. There were no people on the street. It wasn't just the cold – people in Kirby don't walk. In a city that is approximately 1.3 square miles, everyone gets around by car. A few of the younger folks run for exercise. From time to time, someone might walk their dog, though many people just seemed to let their dogs run free off leash. Walking to get from Point A to Point B was rare. Walking, like Jim was now, to clear your head was almost unheard of. Other Kirbyites must not have such cluttered heads, he figured.

"Jim. Ya, over here?"

The newspaper man had been lost in thought and had failed to notice a short redhead in the driveway beginning the arduous climb into her pickup. "Oh, hi Andrea," he said, returning her wave.

Instead of climbing into the truck, Andrea Dhuyvetter closed the door and headed over to Jim. "It should probably run for a minute first. How are you?"

"Can't complain." Jim stopped at Andrea's white picket fence, with her on the other side.

"Well, you could but who'd listen, right?" Andrea smiled and admired the sky. "I wonder if it's going to be another bad one. I don't know how much more I can take, you know."

"It's still early. Winter hasn't even hit yet."

"Oh, I just mean everything. Storms, politics, death."

"Ya."

Andrea Dhuyvetter had been one of the few people in Kirby, North Dakota that Claudette had considered a friend. Andrea was one of the biggest fish in this particular pond: city councilwoman, volunteer ambulance driver and EMT, president of the Women of the Moose, and like Ryan Peterson, owner of a successful insurance agency. Claudette had needed someone besides her husband and kids to talk to, but she always subtly felt that she was better than everyone else in Kirby. Claudette latched onto Andrea. Andrea represented the best of Kirby; that was better than nothing.

Jim wondered if Claudette still kept in touch with her Kirby confidante. Andrea had never given Jim any indication that she knew about the separation, but that didn't necessarily mean anything. Andrea was discreet by nature.

"Is the investigation going well, then?"

"I've decided to leave all of that to the sheriff's office. I was a little out of my element."

"Well that's fine, I'm sure," Andrea tried to sound reassuring. She smiled and said, "I guess there's no point in asking my follow-up question then."

"What was that?" Jim asked in spite of himself.

"Just, whether you think Calvin and Bud Legaard's deaths are related."

Jim's feet turned to mush. He held onto one of the fence's pickets for support.

27

The Sunday night poker game had been instituted by Tor Bakke a year after he was elected sheriff for the first time. The purpose of the game was to have a night where he and his deputies got together and didn't talk about work for once, dammit.

That was the night's one rule: no work talk. And in eight years of poker nights, that rule had never been broken. Also in those eight years, there had not been a murder in Clark County. So this was a week of firsts all around.

"You got anything concrete on these murders yet?" Tor asked Aidan when there was a break in game play. The other deputies who had been exchanging crude jokes were struck dumb by this breach in protocol. Aidan had not been on the force long enough yet to realize the gravity of this moment.

"I don't know if we should be talking in the plural just yet. Bud's death may very well have been accidental." Aidan shuffled the cards.

The sheriff took a drag of his cigarette. His wife Val didn't allow him to smoke in the house during the week, but on Sunday nights all bets were off. "We should know in the morning," the sheriff exhaled. "The guys in Williston are rushing this for us. But I already know what they're going to say. Bud was poisoned. By the same guy who killed Cal. I can feel it in my gut." And it was a considerable gut at that.

"Bud wasn't stabbed, though, like Calvin was." Aidan pointed out.

Tor had considered this. His answer came quickly: "Bud was older, weaker. The poison was enough to do him in. To kill the mayor, he had to be stabbed as well."

That answer actually made some sense to Aidan. Since this case had started, he'd begun to look at Tor as an incompetent country bumpkin with a Norwegian accent. It was likely not a fair assessment.

"So again, I'll ask: do you have anything concrete yet?" Tor's eyes were fixed on him. Aidan looked around; the other three deputies had become intensely fascinated with the composition and structure of the table top.

"We've established a pool of suspects. We've been able to eliminate some. Established a solid timeline for everybody's where-"

Tor pounded his fists onto the table. "An arrest. I'm talking about an arrest. There should be someone behind bars by now. You should have been gathering facts, collecting evidence. Instead you're stopping at every house in town and harassing law-abiding men and their wives." Aidan had an idea as to which wife in particular Tor was referring. The sheriff's face had grown red and his voice was just below a yell. "This is over. I'm putting you back on regular duty."

Aidan let the silence linger for a few moments. He wanted to make sure the sheriff was finished with his tantrum. "Sir," when he finally spoke, he did so softly, "every murder case is different. Sometimes the culprit is obvious and can be arrested the same day. Other cases take weeks. Months." *Some take years and some are never solved*, Aidan thought but chose to keep those off of the list.

"We're not waiting months for you to bring in a killer."

"And you shouldn't. I'm very close. I know it. It won't take months, but I do need more time."

"It's already been decided, Deputy Gray. Investigators from the Williams County sheriff's office will come up on Wednesday to officially take over the case. Maybe stop this guy before he kills a third man."

The air left the room. Aidan prided himself on being a fighter, but there was no fight left in him. This satisfied Tor Bakke a great deal.

Having won the war, he added magnanimously, "You can keep working on it until they get here."

28

Jim began the Monday meeting. On Monday mornings, the staff of *The Kirby Crier* meet at the back table to go over what stories, ads, community announcements and other miscellany they'll be working on for the next two days to complete Wednesday morning's newspaper.

Jim starting by informing Toni, Layla and Brian that he would be back to his normal availability. No more work on the Calvin Lystad investigation for him. They were pleased.

Jim ran down his list of stories. "Doc Haugenoe is done. I still have to write about Friday night's game. The story about the mayor is done."

"Do you need to put something in there about Bud?" Toni asked.

"We'll write it as a separate piece. We don't have proof that they're connected."

"They're not," Layla asserted. "Crazy old man was always wandering around. It was only a matter of time before he froze to death." It seemed a cold thing to say, but she did not say it with coldness.

"Brian, I'll have you write that up." Jim could detect the subtle aroma of put-out-ed-ness that Brian exuded. But he didn't say anything, so that was good. "What have you got?"

Brian consulted his list. "That fire safety thing. Talk about putting in metal detectors at the school. Won't happen. Oh, and the state released a new oil impact study. I can make something out of that."

"And you were working on a water plant story." Jim was referring to the note that Brian had left for him on Friday.

Brian shrugged. "Didn't turn out to be anything." Jim didn't want to believe that Brian had fabricated the whole thing just to get out of covering an old man's birthday party. But he did believe it.

There were a few more items of business and then the meeting was dismissed. Jim asked Brian to hang back a minute while the ladies returned to the front.

"What's up, Jim?"

"We almost missed Doc's birthday party."

"I left you a note."

"At a time when I specifically told you that I wouldn't be around to help out."

"Sorry. I guess it didn't occur to me. I just left you a note, like I'm used to doing."

"Maybe we should change that. From now on if you need me to cover one of your stories, speak to me directly."

"Sure, Jim. Anything else?"

He had more to say, but he thought better of it. "That's it."

Brian nodded, then started for the front. He got three steps in, when Jim thought better of his previous better thinking. "Actually," he called out. Brian turned back around, but didn't approach. This required Jim to talk a little louder, loud enough for the girls to hear in the front if they were trying to listen in. That was fine with Jim.

"Actually," Jim continued, "I've been doing an awful lot of covering for you. Too much. It needs to stop."

"Sure, Jim." Brain made the few steps back to the table.

"You say that," Jim kept his voice up, "but then tomorrow you're going to say you can't cover the Sons of Norway banquet or the ribbon cutting at the new hair place. I can't run this newspaper and write it all by myself Brian."

Jim gave Brian space to say something. He did not. "The new policy is: If you can't cover a story, cover it anyway."

Jim dismissed his employee, then went outside through the back door. He stood there by the door, the snow from last night's storm up to his shin. The temperature was in the low 20s; Jim didn't have a coat on. He was burning hot.

As the morning went on, *The Crier* returned to its usual Monday proceedings. Brian writing the last of the stories for the main news pages, Jim editing those articles and also writing the stories for the sports page, Layla designing the ads, and Toni collecting and transcribing obituaries and news that came in from the surrounding smaller towns. To Jim's relief, life was returning to normal. Maybe even better than normal; Brian seemed to be working a touch harder now.

From time to time, customers came in. Edith Andrist needed a fax sent out because the machine at the nursing home was still on the fritz. A young truck driver who worked for a company that transports water to the oilfield got copies of some maps. Mickey Kilroy wanted to know if it was too late to get an ad in this week's paper. It wasn't. (The deadline is – and has always been – 11 a.m. on Monday if you care to know.) Lars Whalon just wanted to shoot the breeze with Jim, since there was no one at Kirby Auto Parts except his assistant Lee, and Lars didn't find Lee to be the greatest conversationalist. Jim chatted with Lars for a few minutes and then confessed that they were kind of slammed with work trying to get the paper out and could he stop by later. Lars ya'd and made his way back to his store.

Brian was finishing up a phone call when the town's air raid siren went off, providing its daily alert to the usually quiet town that it was noon. Layla was out like a flash. "Just talked to Deputy Tim Aarons," Brain informed the two remaining staff members. "Bud Legaard's cause of death. He froze."

"So it didn't have anything to do with the mayor?" Toni seemed disappointed.

"Ah, the cold is what killed him. But he was also poisoned."

"Rhubarb?" Jim asked.

Brian nodded. "And lye."

"That can't be a coincidence," Toni said.

"Has anyone gotten the mail this morning?" Jim asked. Toni was the only person who ever pick up the mail – usually once in the morning and once in the afternoon. Toni Fager-bakke was 'anyone.'

"Not yet. I'm a little behi-"

"I'll get it," Jim grabbed the key to the P.O. Box and the bag that Toni used to haul the mail.

"Thanks," Toni said suspiciously.

Before Jim could leave, Lois Pedersen entered the building. "Jim," she said. She had aged ten years during the past week, and Lois was no spring chicken to begin with. She held a small leatherbound notebook which she pressed to her chest like a security blanket. He doubted that she was here to make copies.

"Let's go in the back," Jim said.

They sat in silence at the conference table. Jim decided to let Lois take the lead. She obviously was not here to shoot the breeze. No one had really seen her since word had gotten out about her affair with the mayor. Whatever brought her here now was more important than saving face.

Lois gathered up her strength. She set the leather notebook down in front of her. "When Calvin...when the mayor was ki... when he died, I lied and told that deputy the mayor didn't keep a written schedule." She set her hands on the notebook. "I stole his calendar. I didn't want people to see that...I didn't want certain information to get out. But it has anyway. It always does, I suppose."

She slid the book over toward Jim. "Here, then. Maybe there's something in there that will help you find the monster who did this."

"Lois, you should give this to the sheriff."

She shook her head. "I don't like Tor Bakke and he doesn't like me."

"Then take it too Deputy Gray."

"I don't know him. This whole thing is already embarrassing enough. I'm not going to subject myself to more. I brought it to you since you're a friend. You do what you want with it."

Jim had a hard time processing the idea that he and Lois were friends. They'd had many dealings in their professional capacities – some friendly, some downright hostile, most tepid – but the Rosdahls and the Pedersens never paid each other social calls. But the rest of what she said made sense to Jim.

"I'll take this to them for you. They won't need to know where I got it."

Lois didn't smile, but her frown eased. "They'll want to."

"I'm a newspaper editor. I have the right to protect my sources." Lois looked uneasily toward the front office. "They're good about keeping things quiet," Jim said, hoping it was true.

Jim opened the notebook. It was a month-at-a-glance calendar. Random letters had been written down into many of the squares. It was all gibberish to Jim.

"This is all gibberish to me."

"Calvin had a system," Lois said. The system was not complicated. An uppercase 'M' denoted a face-to-face meeting, while an uppercase 'C' denoted a phone call. The lowercase letters below that were usually the initials of the person Calvin was meeting with.

Jim flipped through the pages. He noticed that three or four times a week, Calvin Lystad usually had an 'M' with 'lp.' These were surely his rendezvous with Lois. These three little letters hardly seemed that incriminating. Calvin hadn't exactly written sonnets to his forbidden love. In fact, the two worked together; Jim doubted that anyone would bat an eyelash when they saw that they were having weekly "meetings."

"No locations listed for any of these."

"Ya. Calvin kept that in his head. These were just memory joggers for him."

Jim turned the calendar to October. Two Ms were listed on the day of Calvin's death. There was the "cc" at 7:30, which Jim took to mean "city council." And...

"Who's 'ma'?" Jim asked. "Or is that 'na'?" Calvin did not have the greatest penmanship. Lois did not know who the mystery person was. "Calvin was supposed to meet with 'na' at 6:30. I wonder if na is who killed him."

Jim flipped back to January. Calvin had been to a lot of Ms and had taken many Cs. It would be impossible, and most likely a waste of time, to try and decipher them all. Instead, he looked for patterns. He looked through February and March. There had been no other meetings with na or ma. Other than city council meetings and sex, the only constant was a weekly appointment with 'wl.' Sometimes these were meetings, more often phone calls. Always on Thursday. Jim flipped through the other pages. The appointments continued through the end of July and then stopped completely.

"Calvin didn't tell you who 'wl' was?"

Lois shook her head. Jim felt agitated. Not only did he not know what these letters meant, he didn't even know whether knowing them would actually help the case or not. Jim reminded himself that he wasn't on this case anymore. This wasn't his puzzle to solve. That knowledge gave him little comfort.

29

After Lois left, Jim placed the notebook in the bottom drawer of his desk. He looked at his watch and saw that it was still not quite 12:30. Candy wouldn't have gone to lunch yet. Jim grabbed the box key and bag.

Outside, he looked down Main Street and saw a sheriff's office vehicle outside the Burger Shack. A week before, all of the sheriff's vehicles looked alike to him; but now he knew that this was Aidan's car. Jim considered going back to get the calendar and bringing it to him. But no, he should probably bring it directly to Tor. Besides, Jim had another errand at the moment.

Jim trotted across the street and two doors down to the post office, almost falling once on a patch of ice on the street. Jim entered the lobby which contained the mailboxes for the entire city. It was always open. Near the lobby entrance was another glass door that led into the room where Candy mailed your letters, handed you the packages that wouldn't fit in your box, and told you what was going on in the world. Jim pulled on the door and was glad it hadn't been locked for the lunch half hour yet.

The door would have been locked two minutes earlier but Candy was still trying to invite her last customers to leave. Ardis Knutson was holding onto the counter when Jim entered. Ardis Knudsvig stood behind her, holding a package.

"In my entire life, I've never locked my front door," Ardis Knutson told Candy. "But I did last night."

"Hello, Jim," Ardis Knudsvig twinkled.

"Seems to be warming up," Jim offered as a greeting.

"Sorry, Jim, I'm closed until one," Candy said. "Ardis was

my last customer before lunch."

"That's fine."

If Ardis Knutson heard this hint, she ignored it. "We have got a serial killer on our hands." She turned toward Jim. "Is that what you think? It's a serial killer. In Kirby."

"I don't," Jim said.

The flat dismissal disappointed Ardis Knutson. She said she'd better get going. Everyone exchanged a pleasant good-bye, then Ardis and the other Ardis were out the door.

"How's that grandbaby coming along?" Candy asked after the ladies left.

"Still percolating." Jim made for the door.

"And Claudette?"

Jim closed his eyes to think. This playing coy routine had built up so much pressure inside Jim, he was about ready to pop. Jim opened his eyes and turned back to the counter. If Candy Gillund was on another fishing expedition, she was about to catch a whopper.

"Ya, I do not know," Jim confessed. "We don't really talk these days. Claudette left me."

The room fell still. Then Candy reached under the counter and pulled out a large ring of keys. She rifled through it till she found the one she wanted. She handed the ring to Jim. "Lock that door. You don't need everyone knowing your business."

Jim locked the door, then handed the keys back. He proceeded to unburden himself just as he had with Aidan the week before. It wasn't a very Norwegian thing to do, but it brought some comfort to his soul. He felt confident that the news would be all over town by the evening, but maybe not. At this moment Candy was nothing but empathetic and encouraging. After a few minutes of verbal diarrhea, Jim composed himself and thanked Candy for listening.

"I guess this means I'll have to find someone else to help with the lutefisk dinner," Candy said with a smile in her voice. As ever, the smile did not make its way to her face.

"Afraid so," Jim said as he grabbed the keys to unlock the door.

"What did you want, then?" Candy asked. Jim didn't seem to understand the question. "I assume you had another reason for coming over here."

"Oh ya! I had a question about Bud Legaard. Was he having his mail forwarded to Arizona?"

"Nope. It's been piling up in his box," Candy said.

"When was the last time he picked it up?"

"Thursday," Candy said, "maybe Wednesday. Does that mean something for the case?" she asked.

"I don't know if it means anything. Word around town was that Bud was leaving for Arizona just about the time he died."

"I hadn't heard that."

"It doesn't matter anyway, because I'm not on the case anymore, anyway."

Candy clucked. "Sure, you're not."

30

Toni stopped typing. Through the large front window, she watched her boss step out into the street on his way back toward *The Crier*. He quaked a bit on a patch of ice but quickly recovered. He bounded onto the sidewalk, nearly ran to the door, and opened it. Toni watched this entire scene with one question in her mind.

"Where's the mail?" she asked.

Jim laughed. He looked down at the mailbox key and the empty bag in his hand. "I forgot it."

"You were gone for twenty minutes. What were you doing?"

More laughter. But this time it was coming from Brian. He set the phone receiver down, shaking his head. "Tor Bakke just called."

"He called us?" Jim was intrigued. Usually, they had to hunt down the sheriff's office to get needed information. The authorities rarely reached out to them.

Brian nodded. "Wanted to let Jim know that his presence is formally requested at the inquest for Calvin Lystad and Bud Legaard."

"Inquest?"

"What's that?" Toni asked.

"Tomorrow night at the elementary school. Deputy Aidan Gray will be conducting one last interview with the 'persons of interest' in the case together before turning the investigation over to Williams County."

"Is that a joke?" Jim's gravity was in stark contrast to Brian's levity.

"Most asinine thing I've ever heard of. Is it a joke? Yes. But is it happening anyway? Yes."

Jim did an about face and went back outside. This time Toni watched him speed down the sidewalk, heading south.

Jim's momentum took a hit when he entered the Burger Shack and saw Aidan with that cute Smith girl who worked at the Abstract. He had expected to find Aidan eating alone or with another deputy. Instead, he discovered that Mr. Gray and Ms. Smith were on a date. Jim found budding love alternately endearing and nauseating. At the moment, the pendulum settled on endearing. It was encouraging to know that even in a small town like Kirby it was still possible for two non-Norwegians to find each other.

They were doing that annoying thing that young couples do, where they both sit on the same side of the booth. Aidan was occupied with removing an eyelash from Autumn's face in a smiley and cutesy manner, so he did not see his former "partner" approach. Jim slid onto the empty bench.

"Don't do this," Jim got right to the point.

Aidan straightened up. "Jim, what's wrong?"

"Don't turn this case into a circus."

"Jim, you don't understa-"

"Let me say my peace. If you know who did it, just arrest him. There's no reason to make a spectacle of this. Calvin Lystad and Bud Legaard were not perfect men – God knows – but they deserve better than this." Jim had given this impassioned speech to the table top. He now looked up at Aidan.

"Have you finished saying your peace?"

"Nah. One more thing: I'm surprised, quite frankly. I would have thought this kind of stunt was beneath you. I figured," here Jim stopped himself as he came to a realization. "Uff da, this wasn't your idea, was it?"

Aidan shook his head slowly.

"Tor?"

"I haven't solved anything, Jim. The Williams County sheriff is taking over. Tor wants to 'get some real detectives on this. Folks who can actually find a killer.' Maybe he's right."

"An inquest?"

"That's what he's calling it. It's an embarrassment, I know. He wants to punish me for questioning his wife about the case."

Several arguments came to Jim at this time. In the first place, no one should be above the law. If Val Bakke might be a material witness in a murder trial, they had every right to question her. Secondly, the questions they had posed to her had been softballs, thrown underhanded. They'd never hinted that they considered her a suspect. Thirdly, she didn't answer any of their questions anyway. Fourthly, this was a severe abuse of Tor's power and they should probably contact a lawyer. Jim made none of these arguments.

Instead, he said, "Well, that doesn't give us much time to find the killer."

Aidan smiled. "I thought you were off the case, Columbus."

"It's Columbo. And we both know I'm on the case."

31

Jim left the Burger Shack and started back toward *The Crier*. Despite the two men's zeal, the investigation would have to wait. Jim had a newspaper to put together, and Aidan was about to start a double shift doing traffic stops along Highway 2 (another punitive measure from Tor Bakke). Jim noticed a familiar face across the street and decided to make a little detour on his way back to work.

Ryan Peterson, insurance agent and city councilman, was standing outside the Prairie Land Drug Store. Whenever the weather cooperated – and sometimes when it didn't – the Prairie would set up a table outside of their store and place some of their discounted items on it. When Jim reached Ryan, he was examining a box of off-brand oat bran cereal.

"It's a little cool to have the table out," Jim started the ball rolling.

"No wind, though," Ryan responded rather coolly.

"Don't usually see you out during the day. Things must be slow at work."

Ryan set down the box of cereal. "The opposite. I'm up to my eyeballs in crop insurance claims. With this early snow, farmers didn't get all their acres planted." Ryan picked up another box and examined it. "Every single one of these is expired."

"Must be why they're on sale."

Ryan shook his head. "I worked for a grocery store in Grand Forks back in college. When food expires, you have to throw it out. I guess they figure not a lot of FDA inspectors are going to make it up here."

"Throwing out food? They'll make you turn in your Norwegian card for that, don't ya know?" Jim laid the accent on thick with a smile.

Ryan did not smile back.

Jim moved on. "I thought land deals might be what was keeping you busy."

This time Ryan did smile. It was a large, disingenuous smile that brought all his age wrinkles into view. "I'm not sure I know what you mean."

"Just seems like everyone around here is obsessed with land and mineral rights. Bud Legaard. Calvin Lystad. You?"

"Jim, I have my hands full enough being a business owner and a councilman. And the family. I don't have the time or the inclination to bother with all that."

"Calvin had the time and he was the mayor."

Ryan broke from his usually composed manner. He rolled his eyes. "Uff da, the mayor," he said. "Calvin's the mayor. He's so important." Ryan recovered himself and turned his focus back to the boxes and bags of expired food. "Listen. Being mayor of this town isn't rocket science. It isn't even an overwhelming commitment. A few hours here. A few there. And there's no money in it. You don't become mayor of Kirby because it's a career move. You do it for one of two reasons: you're on some misguided power trip or you're corrupt. Calvin was corrupt."

Jim considered Ryan Peterson a friend, though Ryan was always a bit guarded around him. But hell, half the people in this town were guarded. But double hell, Jim was guarded himself. Jim had never really experienced this side of Ryan and wasn't sure he wanted to.

"Which are you, Ryan?"

"What's that?"

"Are you power hungry or are you corrupt?"

Ryan put his politician smile back on and faced Jim. "I'm just here to serve. The exception that proves the rule."

"Of course. And Jon? And Andrea?"

"Ya. I'm sure." Ryan leaned in and spoke low. "Though confidentially, I wouldn't be surprised if it turned out Councilwoman Dhuyvetter were working with Cal on some land scheme."

"Why do you say that?"

Ryan returned to his full and locked upright position. "Oh, I'm sure she's wasn't. But if it came out that she was, it wouldn't surprise me. That's all I'm saying."

"So she's one of the corrupt ones." Jim did not phrase it like a question.

"That's something you'd need to ask her, I'm sure."

32

After work, Jim decided to make a few house calls. He went first to Jon Knutson's place, where he shared some bars with the councilman and his wife, Heather. Their discussion was comfortable but far from enlightening. Calvin was a difficult personality who had been a bit power crazy. Each of the council members had some vague sense that Calvin was up to something after the eminent domain case; but Jon didn't know what it was. He suspected that the others didn't have any concrete facts about it either. Jon had not hated the mayor, but he didn't really like him either. He got on well with both Andrea and Ryan. The latter sometimes swung on the side of delusion. As had the mayor.

At one point, Jim slipped in – rather slyly, he thought – an offhanded comment about the rhubarb that had poisoned both Calvin and Bud. This was not a fact that had been released yet, so Jim imagined he might be able to use it to his advantage. He'd trick someone into talking about the poison, information only the killer could know. It worked all the time on *Murder, She Wrote*.

"They were poisoned?" was Jon's response. A genuine reaction, by Jim's guess. "Rhubarb is poisonous?"

His next stop was a return visit to the house of the widow Lystad. Hazel was just sitting down to dinner and invited Jim to join her. He graciously declined the offer at first, but Hazel demanded that he stay. She still had a fridge and freezer full of these infernal condolence dinners, and she would never be able to finish them on her own. The grievance tater tot hot dish was already in the oven, so Jim acquiesced.

Having dispensed with the pleasantries about the weather, she was the one who got down to business. "I assume you stopping by means I'm still a suspect."

Jim had just shoved a whopping forkful of the tater tot/wet ground beef/colorless green bean mixture into his mouth. He lifted up a finger while he chewed, the international sign of "hang on a sec."

She did not hang on a sec. "Not that I am a shocked. I come off a little cold, I think." She had a small bite of her own food. "Uff da. This is terrible. Has no one in this town ever heard of paprika?"

"I really just came by to see if you could clarify a few things."

"What would those things be?"

"How much did you know about your late husband's business dealings?"

Hazel huffed at that. "Business dealings. That's grand. Calvin didn't have 'business dealings.' He had stupid schemes. Get rich quick plans. And there were way too many for me to keep track of."

"He didn't talk to you about them?"

"No. I didn't want to know. As long as he kept going after them, that's all I cared about."

Jim scratched his head. "You encouraged these. . . schemes?"

"Ya. It kept him busy. Out in the community. Out of my hair."

"So you don't know about any land deals?"

"I don't know about any deals. I know he was jealous of all of these farmers who've received a fat payday from the oil companies. The Lystads never got any interest on their land. His brother Paul farms the land, but he and Calvin share ownership. Shared" Hazel corrected herself. She finished off her drink. "Oil would have meant a big payday for both of them. Would you like another pop?"

"No," Jim said. Hazel went to the fridge and poured herself another glass of Diet Pepsi. "How jealous?"

"Beyond jealous. He was consumed with it. The Lunds. The Pedersens." The name caught in her throat ever so slightly. "Even your family."

Jim furrowed his brow. His cousin – his mother's brother's son – still managed the farm, but "The Bakke farm doesn't have any oil."

"Well Calvin seemed to think you did," Hazel brushed it aside. "Of course he seemed to think everybody was making out but him. He used to talk with this one oil man. Tried to convince him to take an interest in the land. But he gave up on that a while back."

"How far back?"

"A few months."

"Did this oil man have a name?"

"Most do, now," Hazel said with a shrug. Jim was also sure the oil man had a name. He wondered if that name might not have the initials W.L. "Whatever his name was," Hazel continued, "he seemed a bit shady to me. Specialized in buying up properties that the rest of the companies had passed over. More speculative stuff."

"Do you have a number for this oil man?"

"Calvin did, probably, ya. But I wouldn't have any idea where it is."

"Ya. Cause you didn't know anything about Calvin's doings."

Hazel let out a nervous laugh. "I guess I knew more than I realized."

After dinner came dessert, cherry pie. Jim disliked cherry pie – too sweet – but he disliked being rude even more; so he took his slice without objection. "I'm not a great fan of cherry pie," Hazel confessed, "but I just have to have a change. Everyone gives you rhubarb. If I have one more slice of rhubarb, I'm going to die." Hazel placed her hand over her lips. "My. I suppose that was a poor choice of words."

Jim brightened up. If he wasn't mistaken, Hazel had just

admitted to knowing about the rhubarb poisoning. She had slipped up. Jim felt just like a TV sleuth.

"What's that about rhubarb?" Jim feigned ignorance.

"Don't you know? Calvin was poisoned with rhubarb leaf. That and lye. Bud too. I would think you'd heard that, helping with the investigation and all."

"I did actually. But I'm surprised you did. That information hasn't been released to the public yet."

"Yes it has," Hazel laughed. "Sheriff Bakke released it to Val. And she released it to her good friend, Candy Gillund. And now it has been released to the public."

"Oh." Jim took a bite of pie, dutifully.

"Trying to set a trap for the murderer, Jim?" Hazel asked. He gave his "hold on a sec" sign, but Hazel went on. "I did not kill my husband. I did not love Calvin Lystad, but I did not kill him." Hazel cupped her chin in her hand and looked into the distance, past Jim. The time for confession had come at last; the audience for that confession was irrelevant to Hazel. "We were very young when we married. I was only sixteen. Calvin, nineteen. I loved him in the beginning. Or maybe I was too young to know what love was then. If Calvin ever loved me, I don't know. Maybe he did in his way. He was so young when his mother died and he was looking for a woman to replace her. But his mother was cold, withheld affection. She loved Paul. And she thought the sun rose and set around Peter. But she resented her youngest son, for reasons that only she knew. It was completely unhealthy, but it's what Calvin knew. And it's the kind of relationship he wanted from me. In the end, it's what I gave him."

Confession over, Hazel recovered herself. The faraway look was gone. Her right hand instinctively cinched the top of her blouse, as if covering her shame. "Uff da. Look how I go on. I didn't realize how late it was getting. You must take some pie for the road."

Moments later, Jim stood on the small porch outside Hazel

Lystad's house with an entire rhubarb pie in one hand and what remained of the cherry pie in the other. "Uff da."

33

It was just after 8:00 when Jim left the Lystad home. He decided he had time to pay one more visit.

Jim parked in the street in front of Councilwoman Andrea Dhuyvetter's house. As he walked through the front yard, he thought of all the other times he had made this trip. Jim and Claudette had shared many meals, game nights, and movie nights with Andrea in her house. He hesitated at the door. *That experience will never happen again*, Jim thought.

Jim knocked on the door and heard movement within the house. From his periphery, he noticed a fluttering of the curtain in the nearby window. Someone seeing who was at the door. A safe precaution, but an irregular one around these parts, where many people still didn't even lock their doors. There were more sounds from within. Frantic movements, in Jim's unprofessional opinion. He knocked again.

"Andrea, it's Jim."

"Ya. Hi, Jim. I'll be right there," came Andrea's voice, sounding harried. *What is she doing in there?* Jim thought. This was followed by an unsettling answer. *She's hiding evidence. Burning the paperwork that linked her to a land deal with Calvin Lystad.*

Jim tried to turn the knob. Locked. "Councilwoman Dhuyvetter," Jim shouted. The volume of his voice coupled his banging on the door with his forearm would surely arouse the attention of the neighbors, but Jim was too worried about what was happening inside to worry about what people outside would think. "I need you to come to the door right now."

"Just a moment."

"Now, Andrea." Jim shouted. He was still banging on the

door, while contemplating stepping back and attempting to break it down.

The door flew open. A disheveled Andrea Dhuyvetter looked at Jim in dismay. With a towelette in one hand, she was frantically wiping away the leave-on nighttime beauty cream from her face; with the other hand she was reaching for one of the curlers in her hair. She had already removed about half of the curlers, leaving her red hair flying off in myriad directions.

"What's wrong, Jim? What's happened?"

Jim looked at Andrea in all of her unkempt glory. He laughed. Andrea dropped her hands from her head. "Well, that's a fine 'how do you do'." She ushered Jim inside the house.

After the dust settled, Andrea brewed a pot of coffee for the two of them. "I shouldn't have caffeine this late at night," she said. She took a seat in the wingback chair opposite the couch where Jim stared at his coffee. The remaining curlers had been removed from her head now, save one in the back that she had failed to find. "But old habits die hard."

Jim took a sip of coffee, but the taste of it did not register with him. "Good," he said anyway.

"Thank you. French press. That's the way my father taught me to make it." She luxuriated over her own cup. "You want to explain what happened outside just now?"

"I was worried you were hurt or something when you didn't answer right away."

Andrea lowered her cup and focused on Jim. "I bet. You thought I was up to something. Destroying evidence maybe?"

"You have a very vivid imagination, Ms. Dhuyvetter."

"Ya, I think it's you who has the vivid imagination, Mr. Rosdahl."

Jim asked Andrea some questions about Bud. Andrea told Jim that she didn't know Bud very well; a fact that Jim already knew. Bud did life alone. No wife. No children. Bud didn't have a lot of friends – neither Jim nor Andrea could name one, in fact – or even siblings or extended family as far as anyone was aware.

Jim asked about the eminent domain fiasco.

"Bud forced us into a corner with that one," Andrea insisted. "We needed the land. We offered to buy it from him. He wouldn't sell. We offered him nearly double the market value for it. And with real estate skyrocketing the way it was, that was a princely sum, you know." Andrea took a sip of coffee.

"So you decided to take the land instead?"

"I don't like that word 'take.' We still paid him for it, although not as much as if he'd been willing to work with us. It was for the good of the city. I really believe that."

"Did Calvin believe that?"

"He's the one who presented the idea. He said he'd done some digging into the laws and ordinances. We were within our rights to make the claim. But-." Here Andrea stopped herself.

"But, what?"

"I hate to speak ill of the dead. But I think Calvin took great joy in it. The rest of us went along because our backs were up against the wall; but Calvin treated it like a great victory. Like a personal triumph."

The two sat in silence for a few moments. Those moments were pleasant for Andrea as she enjoyed her coffee and the company of an old friend. Those moments were less so for Jim who was warming up to ask another question."

"Do you own much property?"

"Just this place. You think that I was in on some kind of scheme with the mayor?"

"I've heard it's a possibility."

Andrea smiled. "Yes, when you talk to Ryan Peterson the world is full of possibilities."

"What makes you think-"

"That man is something else. He looks at me as his rival for some insane reason. We're both insurance agents. We're both involved in local politics."

"Those sound like the makings of a rivalry."

"Jim, counting Ryan and me, there are at least five insurance agent in Kirby. We may have one grocery store and no traffic lights, but we have no shortage of insurance agents. A farming community, there is no shortage of people who need to be insured. I'm not a threat to Ryan's business, and he's not a threat to mine."

"What about political rivalry?"

"Ya, ya, no. I wouldn't be mayor of Kirby if Jesus walked across Lake Sakakawea to come ask me himself. I want to serve, but that job's more trouble than it's worth. Ryan can have it, then."

Jim laughed at this. Andrea had that trademark twinkle in her eye that he had seen many times before. Though he couldn't remember ever noticing before what an attractive woman Andrea was, night cream smears along the jawline and all. The two enjoyed their coffee as conversation moved on to less investigatory matters.

34

Tuesday. The newspaper came together without incident. It was one of those rare Tuesdays that found no major storm clouds break and no great fires needing to be put out. Almost all of the stories had been completed the day before; all that remained was to lay out the news pages. Sheriff Tor Bakke failed to get back to Jim about any changes to his Calvin Lystad story. Whether this was due to the sheriff having no issues with the piece or simply an oversight on his part, didn't matter a whit to Jim. The end was the same: He had managed to retain his editorial control.

Jim never sent Tor the story he'd written about Bud Legaard's death. Although the deaths were surely related, the newspaper treated them as separate stories. Besides, Jim was "off the case" when Bud's body was found. So he was off the hook. Further, the paper made no mention of the inquest which would happen that night.

By 11:00 in the morning, the first completed pages were being sent electronically to the printing press in Minot. The last of the pages made it there just before 12:20. Jim was out the door by 1:00, leaving Brian to compile the online edition of the paper, and giving Toni instructions to call him back immediately if the printer in Minot called with any issues.

Jim came home to find his mother was there cleaning. Gladys's nervous habit worked out great for him. He wasn't much of a housekeeper and upkeep had become quite lackadaisical since Claudette's departure. Jim's mother hadn't shown a great deal of interest in the case up to this point – which didn't necessarily mean that the good Norwegian hadn't been interested in the case – but her current cleansing stint indicated to Jim that she was anxious about this inquest. Jim was right there with her on that one.

"When did I make you rhubarb pie?" Gladys asked, pointing to the dessert on his counter.

"I ate at Hazel Lystad's last night. She sent it home with me."

Gladys harrumphed. "That's my tin. She gave you the pie I made for her. She shook her head and shrugged. She said no more about it, but Jim knew that she interpreted such behavior as a moral failing on the part of the widow.

Aidan came over and the two men sat in the living room, talking, while Gladys cleaned and pretended not to eavesdrop. With two hours until the inquest, they had lots to work through. They still had no prime suspect. "Don't worry," Jim assured him, "I'm a newspaper man. I work best under a deadline. We'll come up with it."

Jim went over the details of his meetings from the previous night, with Jon Knutson, Hazel Lystad, and Andrea Dhuyvetter. Aidan shared that he had met with Abby that morning. He learned that while Calvin Lystad had Abby investigate the properties bordering the Lystad farm as a starting point, eventually he had cast a much wider net.

"Maybe we should take a different tack," Jim said after about an hour of going around in circles. "I think we might be overly focusing on the land thing because that's the only real connection between Calvin and Bud. Is it at all possible that their deaths are unconnected?"

"They were poisoned the same way." Aidan shook his head. "If it were just the rhubarb, I'd say maybe. Unlikely, but maybe. But you're talking about two cases in less than a week involving the ingestion of oxalic acid and lye. People don't just go around eating lye."

"Unless it's –"

"Yes, except when you're eating that loony-fish."

"Lutefisk. We Norwegians are a hearty lot. We like to gather once a year around the holidays and eat poison together."

"How festive."

Jim smiled. In his joke, he realized he had stumbled onto something, but he wasn't quite sure what it was. It was a distant tune; Jim closed his eyes to concentrate.

"You figured something out, haven't you?" Aidan asked.

He had. "Datura seeds." Jim ran to the bookshelf and grabbed one of the volumes.

"Is that another Norwegian delicacy?"

"It's another poison. They came up the other day when you were over." Jim found the page that he was looking for. "Basswar Indogram. That's him."

"That our killer?"

"Killer or victim. Depends how you look at it."

After some more discussion, the two men said their goodbyes to Gladys and headed out. Jim kissed his mother on the cheek, a sentiment usually reserved for the holidays. For her part, she sent them off with a smile. An indication that she was pleased with their work.

35

"You must be disappointed," Aidan whispered to Jim. The two men were standing in the entryway of the Kathleen Rosdahl room, the large room at the elementary school where the city council usually held their meetings. They were surveying the folks who had already entered and taken their seats.

"Why would I be disappointed?"

"This is the murder mystery jackpot. You've solved the case and now all of the suspects are gathered in one room. Only, you don't get to present the grand monologue. I do. It must be disappointing."

"Not at all," Jim said. Aidan didn't believe it for a second. He failed to remember that he was in North Dakota now; not drawing attention to yourself was considered one of the great virtues. Aidan, in contrast, enjoyed being the center of attention – which is why this inquest would prove to be a great disappointment for Tor Bakke – and figured that desire was universal; but North Dakota is a whole other universe.

The virtue of invisibility was understood by the other spectators in the room: Hazel Lystad, Abby Quicke, Arley and Lois Pedersen, Ryan Peterson, Jon Knutson, Andrea Dhuyvetter, Paul and Elizabeth Lystad, Dennis Anderson and Val Bakke. They sat in two rows of chairs facing the center of the room with the same collective prayer, which wasn't "I hope they find the killer," but rather "I hope they don't ask me to say anything." Those spectators were about to be disappointed.

Val Bakke, the sheriff's wife, wasn't so much disappointed as she was mad. Val had protested being forced to attend. She had given Tor the idea for the inquest as a way to punish the deputy – and Jim – for causing her great embarrassment, not to put herself in the position to cause more embarrassment. But her husband had insisted she attend. It wouldn't look right if she were absent from the proceeding. And she might end up having something valuable to add. Besides, didn't she want to see Aidan hoisted on his own petard? (No, all the same, she'd rather be home watching Hallmark Movie Channel.)

The sheriff – proceeding as if these were actual proceedings – called the inquest to order. He spoke to those present about the gravity of their current situation. He thanked each of them for their cooperation in the investigation. He apologized on behalf of the entire department for the inadequate job that had been done to this point to find the killer or killers of Calvin Lystad and Bud Legaard. With that lead in, he invited Deputy Gray to come up and make his presentation.

Aidan went up to the front with purpose, carrying a few file folders and the late mayor's date planner, given to him by Jim. Aidan was certain he knew who was responsible for the deaths of Calvin and Bud; but convincing others might not be that easy. But Aidan would not allow uncertainty to cloud his performance. His boss had sought through these proceeding to shame him into kowtowing. That was not Aidan's plan.

He looked to Tor. "Thank you, Sheriff." He turned to those assembled "We are gathered here tonight to unmask a murderer."

There was a slight rumbling within the room. "Okay, okay," Tor said, flapping his hands, "Let's settle down. Just present your facts. We don't need a lot of theatrics."

"Of course, sir," Aidan said theatrically. "As we know, Calvin Lystad was murdered this past Wednesday night. A knife to the chest, after ingesting enough poison to weaken him considerably. Bud Legaard ingested the same poison. Although his frozen body wasn't discovered until Sunday morning, he also died on Wednesday night."

"You don't know that," the sheriff said. "The M.E. couldn't pinpoint the time of death because of the cold."

"An eyewitness, Tomás Escobar, saw Bud staggering off toward the fairgrounds where his body was found. Not knowing what the mayor looked like, Tomás assumed the man was Calvin. But if that had been the case, the man would have been walking in the opposite direction. Toward the theater."

"That still doesn't prove that that's when he was poisoned," Tor returned.

"I can't find one person who saw Bud between Wednesday night and Sunday."

Aidan waited for the next objection. When it did not come, he proceeded. "Let's examine Calvin's death first, since it's the one we've known about the longest. If you could describe Calvin in one word, what would it be?" Aidan turned his focus to Ryan Peterson.

It took a few moments for the councilman to realize the statement was not rhetorical. The question was being addressed to him specifically. "Oh, well. I don't know. I didn't know him all that well."

"You didn't know him well? I thought everyone in Kirby knew everyone else in Kirby really well." This got some smiles from the group. "You served on the city council together. I would think you knew the mayor better than most."

The sheriff, who had been prepared to lean back and enjoy the show, took some pains to sit up. "Deputy Gray. This isn't a court and you're not a lawyer. These are not your witnesses."

"Sir, I apologize. I was merely attempting to ask a few follow up questions of those already interviewed in connection to this case."

"The time for interviews is-"

"Troubled," came a new voice.

The sheriff and his deputy turned from each other to the first row of chairs. "What was that?" Aidan asked.

"If I were to describe Calvin in one word, it would be 'troubled'," Andrea Dhuyvetter said. "That's the nicest way I can say it, I guess. He didn't just want to be mayor. He needed to be mayor. I found that the troubling thing about him."

"Power hungry," Jon Knutson agreed. "That's two words. I hope that's acceptable."

"Now let's don't make this into a free-for-all," the sheriff urged. "We're trying to conduct an official proceeding here. No more questions, deputy."

"He was corrupt, is what he was," Ryan Peterson said. Then he turned to the mayor's widow. "I don't mean to sound hurtful." If Hazel had been hurt by the comment, she showed no outward sign of it.

"Yes, corruption," Aidan picked up the thread. "Everyone I spoke with seemed to have some notion that Calvin Lystad was a corrupt politician."

The sheriff sat back down, but his face indicated his discomfort over the turn things had taken. Aidan continued, "But how exactly was he corrupt? Was it surrounding the hospital tax somehow?" Here Aidan looked squarely at Dennis Anderson, whose bruised face still told the tale of his Friday night altercation with Jim. "Or was it the refusal to support the new daycare?" Aidan took a step in and moved his gaze to Val Bakke. He held his position for just a little too long, before moving on. "Or was his simply a corruption of personal morality?" Here Aidan made sure not to make eye contact with Lois Pedersen or her husband.

"No, the corruption that we're interested in. The one that got him murdered. Was..." Aidan turned to Jim. He felt bad that his partner in this had been relegated to spectator. He was going to bring him into the light, whether the sheriff liked it or not. Or Jim, for that matter.

"Land." The word was spoken resolutely and definitively, but it wasn't spoken by Jim. Hazel addressed the deputy: "That's what all this was about, wasn't it? Land. And oil, of course."

"Calvin was so disappointed when there wasn't any interest in the farm from the oil companies," added the deceased's sister-in-law Elizabeth. Paul Lystad gave a slight nod to show his approval at his wife's words.

The sheriff was out of his seat again. "The purpose of this meeting is for Deputy Gray to make his report, not to replay the entire investigation. If everyone would just remain silent until-"

"The purpose of this meeting," Hazel corrected him, "is to get to the truth of my husband's murder. Sit down now, sheriff, and let us work this out now."

Tor could reprimand Aidan till the cows came home, but there was no correcting Hazel Lystad. Never had been. She was strong, stubborn and had a formidable physical presence. And now the grieving widow had the added advantage of being a sympathetic figure.

"As I told Jim here," Hazel resumed, "Calvin was talking to this man who specializes in long shots. Oh what do you call it?"

"Speculative markets," Jim offered.

"Ya sure."

"But even this speculator didn't have any interest in the Lystad Farm." Jim didn't mind talking now, since he wasn't being forced to stand. This was less like a performance and more like a conversation. Jim could do conversation. "So…"

"He went looking for someone else's land?" Andrea sounded uncertain, even though she knew she had hit the nail on the head.

The inquest had turned into a gab session and Aidan felt suddenly self-conscious about being the only person standing. He grabbed the empty chair next to the sheriff, brought it near to the spectators and had a seat. His back was to Tor now. "The mayor decided to buy up properties cheap," Aidan enjoined. "He would find land that the oil people had passed over, but that this speculator would be interested in. He'd buy the 'worthless' land from the owners and then lease the mineral rights to his man."

"But just the lease wouldn't begin to cover the cost to buy the land," Jon Knutson said. "If Calvin was going to make money on this, at some point they would have to drill. And find something."

"It is a pretty big gamble," Jim agreed. "Too much for him?"

"He would," Hazel said. "I don't have any question about that. Calvin was a risk taker with everything but his health, to be sure. And going in for every get rich quick scheme he found. But what he didn't have – what *we* didn't have – was money. He couldn't have bought any land on our abundant nest egg."

"He needed a partner," Ryan Peterson said. "A money man. Calvin had the connection, someone else fronts the money. They split the payday." Ryan felt the eyes on him and worried they were judging him. "It wasn't me."

Jim was enjoying this interaction. Everyone jumping in. Turning the crime solving into a community effort. This is what small towns did best: Gossip. Maybe they should have gotten together and just talked it out from the beginning.

"Bud," came the unexpected voice of Paul Lystad. The others looked to Paul for more. No more was offered.

"Paul, what about Bud?" Jim asked.

"Bud had plenty of money."

"And land too," Elizabeth agreed. "Bud owned land all over. Never farmed it, never developed it. I don't think he even has any wells on any of it. He just hoarded it. Whenever I'd see him in town, I'd ask him 'Are you ever going to do anything with that big stretch of land you've got north of us?' There are no buildings. No crops. Just land. Going to waste." She concluded her rabbit trail speech with a slow shake of the head. "So sad, you know."

"You think Calvin and Bud were business partners?" Tor asked. Even he couldn't help getting caught up in the current. "But Calvin and Bud hated each other."

"But they didn't, sheriff," Andrea Dhuyvetter corrected

him. "Calvin and Bud got on pretty well until the city council built that road on his land."

"Yes," Ryan agreed. "The evil city council stealing land from a simple old man. We didn't even want the land. We tried to pay him just for the right to build the road. He wouldn't have it – said it ruined his property. Property he didn't live on or even use. So we offered to pay him for the whole parcel. No way, he said. We finally had to declare eminent domain so that he would have to sell it to us."

"But you think they could have been working together prior to that?" Jim asked Andrea.

"I think so. But whatever deal they had never would have survived that fight."

"That's for sure." Val Bakke was sitting off to herself on the end of the second row. She had been determined not to participate in this horrible display. But then, sometimes contributing is the right and neighborly thing to do. "That last council meeting. Well, not the last one, the one where Bud got into a shouting match with Cal. You know which one I mean. Bud saying he's going to call a lawyer and sue his parents and his children."

Aidan was surprised to hear Val's voice; now the entire room was in for a surprise. "Not children," Lois said. "He didn't say anything about children."

"Oh, I'm sure he did," Val insisted. Lois shrugged. She was still walking around town like a wounded cat. She had no interest in getting into an argument.

Jim thought there might be something here to pursue. "How do you remember it, Lois?"

Her husband Arley spoke for her, "She remembers everything. Got one of those photographic memories."

"If I'm concentrating," she amended. "I can remember most things. And I'm always focused at those meetings. Bud said, 'I'll sue you for everything you got, Cal. Sue your entire family. Your wife, your brothers and your mother. Acting so high and mighty. You're not a damn thing. I know where you come from.' Then Calvin. . . then the mayor said, 'Go home, William.'"

Simultaneously, Aidan and Jim straightened in their seats. If life were a cartoon, a large light bulb would have appeared above each of their heads. Both men had heard the final piece of information that made everything else click into place. (It would turn out that they had heard different things.)

"The mayor called him William?" Aidan asked.

"Yes," Lois said, "William was his given name. He hated it, so he gave himself the name Bud. Everyone called him Bud except the mayor."

Aidan went over to the table and retrieved the calendar notebook. He opened it and addressed the city clerk. "Lois, this was the mayor's calendar, right?"

She tightened up. That phantom concern of "what if people find out?" still lingered in her actions. She said with some trepidation, "Ya."

Aidan pointed to a specific spot and brought it close to her. "Could you tell me what this notation on Wednesday, May 7 means?"

Lois barely had to look. "He had a meeting on that day with a W.L." Then a flash of understanding. "William Legaard."

Aidan closed the book and brought it back to the table. "Calvin had meetings with this W.L. once a week, every week for some time, beginning in February. If I'm not mistaken, that's when they began employing your services, Mrs. Quicke."

Abby nodded. She considered not answering. She had worked illegally 'off the books' for Calvin; this admission might get her into some pretty hot water. Though not as hot as the murder. "Mayor Lystad hired me to find out who owned land and mineral rights to an assortment of properties around Clark County."

"Here's what I don't understand," Elizabeth Lystad said. "I never knew Bud to pay any interest to oil. Years ago, he bought all this land dirt cheap; but he just sat on it. He didn't want to get rich. He just liked having property. That land north of us never had a single crop or anything. So sad." She reiterated her earlier lament.

"Maybe Bud had a change of perspective," Aidan suggested.

"Maybe Calvin persuaded that change," Jim seconded.

"Maybe he flat out lied to Bud about what they were doing," Hazel suggested. "He had a way of doing that sometimes."

A low murmur within the crowd seemed to confirm this assessment. Aidan moved on. "Whatever the circumstances, the two had some sort of falling out. The meetings between Calvin Lystad and Bud Legaard ended at the end of July."

Andrea raised her hand like an excited schoolgirl. "That's when the eminent domain stuff happened."

Councilman Ryan Peterson shook his head. "Thirty yards of roadway seems like a petty thing to dissolve a business relationship over. If Calvin and Bud were such pals, though, couldn't he have smoothed things over?"

"He didn't need to," Aidan said. "He didn't need Bud anymore. He'd found the money he needed from someone else." Aidan fixed his gaze on Ryan.

"Me? You can't be serious."

Aidan nodded, then pointed at Jon Knutson. "And you?"

Jon was flabbergasted. "What?"

But Aidan wasn't done; he pointed at Andrea. "You too." She chose deep thinking over defensiveness and after a few seconds hit on what the deputy was saying.

"You mean the city," Andrea said with understanding. "Calvin realized that he didn't need a partner with money. He would use the city's resources to purchase the property."

Jon exhaled. "None of us would go along with him on that."

"I don't know, Jon," Andrea said, "Calvin could have convinced us to take on several properties around town. He makes a solid case for why we have to get ahead of the ball on the city's rapidly growing population. We might go along with it."

"We're not going to go declaring eminent domain every week on another plot," Ryan protested.

"We wouldn't need to. If we were offering people twice what their land is worth, like we did with Bud, they'd jump at it," Andrea said. Jim noticed Andrea tugging on her left earlobe, which she did when she was unraveling an issue. She was unaware of this affectation. "Little by little we realize, 'Hey we don't really need this space' and 'this land we have over here is still a little too remote.' Perhaps Calvin would have offered to take the land off of our hands. We lose out on the deal, but at least we get back something."

Jon had come on board with Andrea. "Then the next month, Calvin has the good fortune to strike oil." This explanation satisfied the group. Smiles and nods all around.

Tor leaned forward in his chair. "But who killed them?" He asked.

"That is the question," Aidan said. He surveyed the room to see if anyone wanted to venture a guess. A few people gave non-verbal indicators that they believed the person in the row behind them or two seats down from them might be the killer. These people were careful not to actually say anything though.

"Don't make sense," Paul said after a good long time. He added a little more time before going on. "Their feud was theirs."

Aidan agreed. "That was our stumbling block as well. Anyone who might want to kill the mayor wouldn't have a motive to kill Bud. And vice versa. The only people involved in this land dispute was the two of them."

"What about this oil man? The speculator?" The sheriff asked.

"Calvin was desperate to get this man interested in what he had, but this guy wasn't on the hook yet. He had no reason to care about any of this until Calvin had something he wanted."

"Deputy," Abby said, "you said that *was* your stumbling block. Meaning it's not anymore? Have you figured out who killed the mayor and Mr. Legaard?"

"I did not," Aidan said. An air that had been breathed into the room a moment earlier, now deflated. "But he did." Aidan pointed to the newspaper man.

All eyes turned to Jim. There was now no air in the room, as the assemblage held their collective breath. Jim felt uncomfortable again. The conversation had turned into a public speaking class. He didn't like this kind of attention.

"Basswar Indogram," is all he said.

Understanding that this was a bombshell, but not understanding what that bombshell was, the people gathered in the Kathleen Rosdahl room at the Clark County Elementary School reacted in the only appropriate way: everyone started talking at once. "Who?" "What's that now?" "Uff da! That a name or something?" "Sounds like one of those oil workers."

The sheriff stood and settled the group down. "Now Jim," he asked, "you mind filling us all in on who this Indo-whatever is?"

"He was an Indian. In the-"

"They're called Native Americans now," Elizabeth was happy to inform him.

"No, he was from India. In the nineteenth century, Basswar went around poisoning strangers with datura seeds and then robbing them. People didn't realize they were eating poison because Basswar would eat some of the seeds too."

"Built up a tolerance," Paul surmised.

"Tolerance or not," Jim continued, "it eventually caught up with him. He ended up poisoning himself to death."

"What does any of this have to do with the price of tea in China?" Ryan Peterson asked.

Aidan spoke up. "Bud was angry. Angry over the breakup of the partnership, angry over his land being bought out from under him, angry because he realized that the mayor might try to do it again. Whatever the reason, Bud decided to kill Calvin. Poison was easiest, but too imprecise. Stabbing would take some of the guess work out of it. Bud was old, though. He wouldn't have the strength to both fend off his victim and stab him to death."

"So he weakened him with the poison," Tor nodded his approval.

"And somehow Bud ended up ingesting the rhubarb leaves as well. Maybe it was an accident. Perhaps he took some as a sign of good faith, and it got to him. However it happened, Bud had enough energy to stab the mayor, before staggering back home. Calvin received a rush of adrenaline when he was stabbed, giving him the strength to get to the theater before collapsing. Bud on the other hand, growing weaker, never made it home." Aidan gave everyone a moment to let this all sink in.

"Yes," he said when Elizabeth raised her hand.

"How do you know that it wasn't Calvin who poisoned Bud and Bud stabbed him in self-defense?"

Hazel turned around to look at her former sister-in-law. "We're talking about Calvin here, Elizabeth."

"Ya, ya, no. You're right. Never mind."

"Now what does that mean?" the sheriff nearly shouted.

"Calvin wouldn't have taken poison – not even a small amount – in order to convince someone else to take a lot. Calvin took risks with his money, with his time, with his integrity. But he would never take a risk with his health. He wouldn't put himself in a situation where he might harm himself."

"Yep. Yep." Paul agreed.

"Also," Aidan said, "the mayor had three times the amount of poison in his system that Bud did."

"So that's it?" Tor asked.

Indeed that was it. Aidan with a little help from Jim had presented the town with their killer. No need to ask any more questions. No reason to hand over the investigation to the men in blue from Williston. No point in more discussion of rhubarb poisoning when everyone had their own rhubarb pies waiting for them at home. The folks who had gathered at the elementary school that night dispersed.

"Congratulations," Jim said to Aidan when they were outside the school. Jim shook Aidan's hand.

"What's wrong?" Aidan asked. Indeed Jim seemed to be somewhere else. "What are you working out in that head of yours?"

"Nothing. It's just been a long night."

"Uff da! Ain't that the truth?"

Jim smiled wide. "Your first 'uff da'. They grow up so fast." Jim wiped a phony tear from his eye.

36

From the school, Jim walked over to his mother's house. He figured that she would have gone back to her own place by now, and he was correct. Gladys Rosdahl reclined in her chair watching an old episode of *Dr. Quinn, Medicine Woman*; the volume was nearly all the way up. Jim sat on the couch.

"How'd it go?" she called out over the din. Jim reached over and took the remote, lowering the volume to a light roar.

"Deputy Gray presented his case tonight."

"Were there a lot of people there?"

"No, thankfully." Jim ran off the names of those in attendance, then summarized the proceedings.

"Well, good," Gladys said when her son had finished his account.

"Yep."

"You don't seem too happy about it."

Jim shook it off. He rose and handed the remote back to his mother. "I'm a little hungry."

"There are bars on the counter."

Jim's body headed toward the kitchen, but his head was somewhere else. He stopped before he reached the kitchen. He closed his eyes tight and stood motionless for a few moments.

When he opened his eyes, he turned and went back to the living room. Jim grabbed the remote, clicked off the television, and sat down. "I just feel a little sick to my stomach. You stand in front of a group of people and say 'Bud Legaard is a murderer.' You're destroying a man's reputation. A dead man, but still." There was a pause as Jim wrestled more with his thoughts. "I say it's okay. Bud doesn't have any family. Not a lot of friends even. The damage to his reputation doesn't really matter. It still makes me sick."

"If Bud did it, then that's all there is to it," Gladys said softly.

"He's not alive to defend himself. Which makes it easier."

"What are you talking about?"

Jim took a long deep breath. "It's not that hard to make a case for murder. Anybody could have done it. 'Dennis Anderson did it. He stabbed Calvin, then went to spend the evening with his lady friend.' It doesn't explain Bud's death, but you figure something out. 'Andrea Dhuyvetter killed them. Tired of Calvin and Bud's schemes, she poisons them both, but it turns out she didn't use enough. Calvin recovers and makes it to the theatre lobby. When she leaves to go to the bathroom she sees him and stabs him to finish the job.' It's not terribly difficult to make a case for a lot of people."

Gladys rose, concern written across her face. "I'm going to get you a bar. You don't look well."

"I could say you did it even."

Gladys sat back down.

"Sure. I could say that you arranged to have both of them over here before the city council meeting. You offer them both a slice of your famous pie. Rhubarb right from your garden. Only this time, you make your pie with a little something extra: the poisonous leaves of the rhubarb plant. Maybe spike your lemonade with lye for good measure.

"If that happened, I would say that the men arrived at two different times. Let's say Bud came first. He has a slice of pie and conversation. The pie makes him sick, but the conversation makes you realize that Bud isn't someone you need to kill. You send him on his way. After that, Calvin shows up. He has a lot of your pie, why wouldn't he, it's very good. Again, maybe not enough poison to kill him, but it weakens him enough that you're able to grab one of your kitchen knives and plunge it into his chest."

"Uff da!" Gladys looked at the blank television screen.

"I know, it's a little crazy. I could say that the stabbing brought Calvin a momentary burst of life. So to speak. He headed out the door. He was disoriented, but he was able to find his way back over to Main Street. The lights of the theater drawing him there. That's where he collapsed and died.

"I could recall how you were cleaning the house when I came over that night. I know you clean when you're nervous, and you were nervous about the meeting. But I could argue that you were cleaning up the blood that would have inevitably dripped while the mayor was here. People around here would find that quite a story. Jim Rosdahl accuses his own mother of murder."

Without looking at her son, Gladys said: "People might want to know what possible reason your mother would have for killing him."

"Without a doubt." Jim stretched out across the couch, feigning ease. "You certainly never seemed to pay much mind to Calvin Lystad one way or the other. You might have an opinion about the things the city council was doing, but none of it affected you personally. It would have to be something else. Maybe something that happened a while ago. An old story that was threatening to be told again.

"But how far back would we have to go? Why not all the way back? To before Calvin was born even. Ole and Mabel have two sons, Paul and Peter. They have a nice little farm that sustains them. But then Mabel falls ill. Doc Haugenoe tells her she's depressed, but Mabel knows better; she has rheumatic fever. She becomes bedridden. Can't take care of her boys. Can't run the household. Like most anyone would do in that situation, Ole turns to his neighbors. The Bakkes have a daughter, Gladys. Only fifteen at the time."

"Fourteen," his mother said, still not looking at him.

"Fourteen. Young, but old enough her dad decides to earn her keep and bring in a little bit extra money for the family. So the daughter moves in with the Bakkes, now: cleaning and cooking, caring for the invalid, taking care of two young children, and their father too."

Jim noticed his mother's body shiver slightly. "And that's where the trouble began. Ole Lystad. He's found someone to cook and clean, but a husband has other needs too. His bedridden wife cannot or will not oblige him. So he turns-"

"Please stop." Gladys wiped her hand across her cheek. Jim didn't see a tear, but it must have been there.

"I need to go on," Jim asserted gently, "but I can skip ahead some. A few months later, this child discovers that she is going to have a child herself. Any number of things could have happened at that point. Ole could have insisted she get it taken care of. Or maybe his high moral fiber made that an impossibility. I'm sure her parents were told at some point. Knowing her father, Amos, I wouldn't be surprised if he hit Ole a few times."

The corners of Gladys' mouth turned upward at the memory. "Mabel wasn't the only one bedridden for that week."

"The Lystads and Bakkes decided to keep the baby a secret. The girl would have the baby; the Lystads would raise the child as theirs. It wouldn't be too hard to pull off. Many babies were born at home back then. And they lived on a farm; it'd be easy enough to hide the girl away until she delivered. The Lystads' other two children were probably still too young to realize exactly what was happening."

Jim sat back up and shrugged. "It's a theory, at least. Usually the youngest child is doted on. Loved more than the others. Not Calvin. Mabel seemed to detest him. It would make sense if he wasn't her son. Not only that; he was a constant reminder of her husband's indiscretion.

"Now we move to present day. Four of the five people who know the truth about Calvin Lystad's origins are dead. The only one who knows is his real mother, who has become a respected and honored woman in her home town. She has every intention of letting the secret die with her.